Jesse still held her hand, and when she made no effort to free it he tightened his grip—now he had her so close he couldn't bear to let her go.

She closed her eyes with a flutter of long fair lashes, and he could feel her tremble beneath his touch as his fingers traced down her cheek toward her mouth.

Her lips parted just enough for her to breathe out a slow sigh, and she opened her eyes. In them were both wariness and want.

"Jesse, I..."

He dropped his hand and used it to take her other hand and pull her closer to him—so close he could feel the heat from her sun-warmed body. He pressed his mouth to hers in a soft, questioning kiss—she gave him the answer he wanted with the pressure of her lips back on his. As he deepened the kiss he felt the same fierce surge of possessive joy he'd felt the first time he'd kissed her. He had kissed her and then lost her through a stupid misunderstanding.

She tasted the same. Felt the same. And he wanted her just as much—more.

Dear Reader,

I'm so pleased to be welcoming you to my third book set in Dolphin Bay, a small coastal town with a quaint harbor and beautiful beaches on the south coast of New South Wales, Australia.

We met Lizzie Dumont and Jesse Morgan in my first Dolphin Bay book, *The Summer They Never Forgot*, and then again in *The Tycoon and the Wedding Planner*. Somehow, although the odds were against these two falling in love, I was determined to get them together!

In *A Diamond in Her Stocking*, Lizzie has put a broken marriage behind her and come to Dolphin Bay to make a new start for her and her young daughter. There's no room in her life for a man—and especially not for a heartbreaker like gorgeous Jesse Morgan, no matter how much he makes her heart race.

The townsfolk have laid bets that movie-star-handsome Jesse will never settle with one woman. But Jesse has his own reasons for having closed off his heart against pain and betrayal.

Lizzie and Jesse are perfect for each other—but there are some big barriers to come down before they can see that and take the risk to trust again. It was such fun helping them get there! I do hope you'll enjoy their story.

Kandy

A Diamond in
Her Stocking

Kandy Shepherd

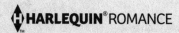

Recycling programs
for this product may
not exist in your area.

ISBN-13: 978-0-373-74319-3

A Diamond in Her Stocking

First North American Publication 2014

Copyright © 2014 by Kandy Shepherd

Printed in U.S.A.

Kandy Shepherd swapped her fast-paced career as a magazine editor for a life writing romance. She lives on a small farm in the Blue Mountains near Sydney, Australia, with her husband, daughter and a menagerie of animal friends. Kandy believes in love at first sight and real-life romance—they worked for her!

Kandy loves to hear from her readers. Visit her website at www.kandyshepherd.com.

Recent titles by Kandy Shepherd:

THE TYCOON AND THE WEDDING PLANNER
THE SUMMER THEY NEVER FORGOT

**This and other titles by Kandy Shepherd
are also available in ebook format from
www.Harlequin.com.**

To the A-team, Cathleen Ross, Elizabeth Lhuede and Keziah Hill, with heartfelt thanks for the friendship and support!

CHAPTER ONE

As Lizzie Dumont looked around at the soon-to-open Bay Bites café, her new place of employment, she vowed she would never reveal how she really felt about the way her high-flying career as a chef had crash-landed into a culinary backwater like Dolphin Bay. Not when people here had been so kind to her.

She would put behind her the adrenalin rush of working at star-rated restaurants in the gastronomic capitals of Paris and Lyon. Give up the buzz of being part of the thriving restaurant scene in Sydney. Embrace the comparatively lowly life of a café cook.

Her sigh echoed around the empty café. Who was she kidding? That heady time in France had been the pinnacle of her career. But she'd been sinking in Sydney. Working shift after shift until past midnight in restaurant kitchens—no matter how fashionable the venues—

had hardly been compatible with being a good parent to her five-year-old daughter, Amy.

With no family in Sydney to fall back on, and few friends because she'd lived in France for so long before her divorce, she'd struggled to give Amy a reasonable life. Drowning in debt, swimming against the current of erratic babysitter schedules and unreasonable rosters, after less than a year she'd been going under.

By the time her sister Sandy had approached her to manage the new café adjacent to Sandy's bookshop, Lizzie had been on the edge of despair. She'd even been contemplating the unthinkable—letting Amy live permanently with her ex-husband Philippe in France.

Gratefully, she'd grabbed the lifeline Sandy had thrown her.

And here she was. Dolphin Bay was a rapidly growing resort town on the south coast of New South Wales, with a heritage-listed harbour and beautiful beaches. It was also, in her experience, a gastronomic wasteland—the only memorable meal she could ever remember eating was fish and chips straight from the vinegar-soaked wrapping.

But Sandy had offered her sanctuary and a new life with Amy. In return, Lizzie would throw herself wholeheartedly into making Bay Bites the best café on the south coast. Heck, why stop there? She would use her skills and expertise to make Bay Bites the best café in the country.

She let herself get the teeniest bit excited at the thought. After all, she would be in charge. No cranky head chef screaming insults at her. No gritting her teeth at an ill-chosen item on the menu she'd been forced to cook whether she'd liked it or not.

She continued her inspection, her spirits rising by the second. Sandy had done a wonderful job of the fit-out. The décor was sleek and contemporary but with welcome touches of whimsy. In particular, she loved the way the dolphin theme had been incorporated. Hand-painted tiles backed the service area. Carved wooden dolphins supported the wooden countertop and framed the large blackboard on the wall behind it where she would chalk up the daily specials.

There was still work to be done. Lots of it. Boxes were stacked around the perimeter of the café waiting for her to unpack. Large flat packages, wrapped in brown paper, were propped against the walls. She itched to get started.

But someone had started the unpacking. Outsized glass jars were already lined up at the other end of the counter to the cash register, their polished chrome lids glinting in the late afternoon sun that filtered through the plate glass windows that faced the view of the harbour.

She could envisage the jars already filled with her secret recipe cookies. Nearby was the old-fashioned glass-fronted rotating cabinet for cakes and pies she'd asked Sandy to order. The equipment in the kitchen was brand new. It was perfect. *She would make this work.*

Lizzie ran her hand along the wooden countertop, marvelling at the intricacy of the carved dolphins, breathing in the smell of fresh varnish and new beginnings.

'Those dolphins are kinda cool, aren't they?' The deep masculine voice from behind her made her spin around. She recognised it immediately.

But the shock of seeing Jesse Morgan stride through the connecting doorway from Bay Books next door expelled all the breath from her lungs. Her heart started to hammer so hard she had to clutch her hands to her chest to still it.

Jesse Morgan. All six foot three of him: black-haired, blue-eyed, movie-star handsome. Jesse Morgan of the broad shoulders and lean hips; of honed muscles accentuated by white T-shirt and denim jeans. Jesse Morgan, who was meant to be somewhere far, far away from Dolphin Bay.

Why hadn't someone warned her he was in town?

Lizzie's sister was married to Jesse's brother Ben. Six months ago, Jesse had been the best man and she the chief bridesmaid at Ben and Sandy's wedding. Lizzie hoped against hope Jesse might have forgotten what had happened between them at the wedding reception.

One look at the expression in his deep blue eyes told her he had not.

She cringed all the way down to her sneaker-clad feet.

'What are you doing here?' she managed to choke out once she had regained use of her voice. She was aiming for nonchalance but it came out as a wobbly attempt at bravado.

'Hello to you, too, Lizzie,' he said with a Jesse-brand charming smile, standing there in her café as confident and sure of himself as ever. A confidence surely bred from an awareness that since he'd been a teenager he would always be the best-looking man in the room. But she noticed the smile didn't quite warm his eyes.

She tried to backtrack to a more polite greeting. But she didn't know what to say. Not when the last time they'd met she'd been passionately kissing him, wanting him so badly she'd been tempted to throw away all caution and common sense and go much further than kissing.

'You gave me a fright coming in behind me like that,' she said with a rising note of defensiveness to her voice. Darn it. That was a dumb thing to say. She didn't want him to think he had any effect on her at all.

Which, in spite of everything, would be a total lie. Jesse Morgan exuded raw masculine appeal. It triggered a sudden rush of awareness that tingled right through her. Any red-blooded woman would feel it. *Lots* of red-blooded women had felt it, by all accounts, she thought, her lips thinning.

'I didn't mean to scare you,' he said. 'But Sandy told me you were in here. She sent me to give you a hand with the unpacking. I've made a start, as you can see.'

He took a step towards her. She scuttled backwards, right up against the countertop, cursing herself for her total lack of cool. She was so anxious to keep a distance between them she didn't register the discomfort of the dorsal fin of the wooden dolphin pressing into her back.

It wasn't fair a man could be so outrageously handsome. The Black Irish looks he'd inherited from his mother's side gave him the currency he could have chosen to trade for a career as an actor or model. But he'd laughed that off in a self-deprecating way when she'd teased him with it.

Which had only made him seem even more appealing.

How very wrong could she have been about a man?

'I only just got here from Sydney, after a four-hour drive,' she said. 'I…I haven't really thought where to start.'

'Can I get you a drink—some water, a coffee?' he asked.

He sounded so sincere. *All part of the act.*

'No, thank you,' she said, regaining some of her manners now the shock of seeing him had passed. After all, he was her sister's brother-in-law. She couldn't just ask him to leave, the way she'd like to. 'I stopped for a bite to eat on the way down.'

Despite herself she couldn't help scanning his face to see what change six months had brought him. Heaven knew what change he saw in her. She felt all the stress of the last months had aged her way more than her twenty-nine years.

He, about the same age, looked as though a care had never caused his brow to furrow. His tan was deeper than when she'd last seen him, making his eyes seem even bluer. A day away from a shave, dark growth shadowed his jaw. His black hair was longer and curled around his ears. She remembered the way she had fisted her hand in his hair to pull him closer as she'd kissed him.

How could she have been so taken in by him?

She squirmed with regret. She'd known of his reputation. But one champagne had led to one champagne too many and all the tightly held resolutions she'd made after her divorce about having nothing to do with too-handsome, too-charming men had dissolved in the laughter and fun she'd shared with Jesse.

Was he remembering that night? How they'd found the same exhilarating rhythm dancing with each other? How, when the band had taken a break, they'd gone outside on the balcony?

She'd been warned that Jesse was a heartbreaker, a womaniser. But he'd been fun and there hadn't been much fun in her life for a long time. It had seemed the most natural thing in the world to slip into his arms when he had kissed her in a private corner of the balcony lit only by the faintest beams of moonlight. His kiss had been magical—slow, sensuous, thrilling. It had evoked needs and desires long buried and she had given herself to the moment, not caring about consequences.

Then a group of other guests had pushed through the doors to the balcony with a burst of loud chatter, and broken the spell.

It had been the classic wedding cliché—the chief bridesmaid and the best man getting caught in a passionate clinch.

Lizzie cringed at the memory of those moments. The hoots and catcalls of the other guests as they'd discovered them kissing. 'Jesse's at it again,' someone had called, laughing.

She'd never felt more humiliated. Not because of being caught kissing. They were both single adults who could kiss whomever they darn well pleased. She'd laughed that off. No. The humiliation was caused by the painful awareness she'd been seen as just another in a long line of Jesse's girls. Girls he had kissed and discarded when the next pretty face had come along.

But, despite knowing that, it hadn't stopped her from going back for more with Jesse that night. Why had she imagined he'd be any different with her?

What an idiot she'd been.

Now she cleared her throat, determined to make normal—if stilted—conversation; not to let Jesse know how shaken she was at seeing him again. How compellingly attractive she still found him.

'Aren't you meant to be gallivanting around the world doing good works? I thought you were in India,' she asked. Jesse worked for an international aid organisation that built housing for the victims of natural disasters.

Jesse shook his head. 'The Philippines this time. Rebuilding villages in the aftermath of a gigantic mudslide. Thousands of houses were destroyed.'

'That must have been dangerous,' she said. Jesse was a party guy personified, and yet his job took him to developing countries where he used his skills as an engineer to help strangers in need. She'd found that contradiction fascinating.

Just another way she'd been sucked into his game.

'Dangerous and dirty,' he said simply. 'But that's what we do.'

She shouldn't feel a surge of relief that he had escaped that danger without harm. But she did. Though she told herself that was just because he was part of the extended family now. The black sheep, as far as she was concerned.

'So you're back here because…?'

'The "good works" led to an injured shoulder,' he said. He raised his broad right shoulder to demonstrate and in doing so winced. His so-handsome face contorted in pain and the blood drained, leaving him pale under his tan.

Her first reaction was to rush over and comfort him. To stroke his shoulder to help ease the pain. Or offer to kiss it better…

No! She forced her thoughts away from Crazyville. Gripped her hands tightly together so she wouldn't be tempted. She was furious with herself. Wasn't she meant to now be immune to his appeal?

Getting together with Jesse Morgan at the wedding had been like nibbling on just one square of a bar of fine Belgian dark chocolate and denying herself the rest even though she knew it would be utterly delicious. Quite possibly the best chocolate she had ever tasted.

But she prided herself on her willpower when it came to chocolate. And men who offered her nothing more than a fleeting physical thrill.

Her aim was to build a new life for her and Amy. She didn't want a man around to complicate things. Not now. Maybe not ever. And if she did decide to date again it wouldn't be with someone like Jesse Morgan. She'd been there, done that, with her good-looking charmer of an ex-husband who had let her down so badly.

The next man for her—if she decided to go

there—would be steady, reliable, living in the same country as her and average-looking. She wanted a man who only had eyes for her.

Jesse was a player and Lizzie didn't want to play. Her party-girl days were far behind her. It would be work, work, work for her in Dolphin Bay. And being the best mother she could possibly be to her precious daughter.

Not that Jesse was giving her any indication that he had a real interest in her. Not now. Not then. It still stung. *How could she have believed in him?*

After they'd been interrupted on the balcony, she'd rushed away to look in on Amy. When she'd returned, out of breath from her hurry to get back to Jesse, she had found him dancing with a beautiful dark-haired woman, his head too close to hers, his laughter ringing out over the noise of the band. Had he taken her out onto the balcony and kissed her too? Lizzie hadn't hung around to find out. She'd avoided him for the rest of the evening.

'I'm sorry to hear you've been hurt,' she said stiffly.

Boy, had she wanted to hurt him back then.

'All in the line of duty,' he said. 'My own fault for grappling with a too-large concrete beam without help.'

'So you've come home to recuperate?' she

asked. She became aware of the carving pressing into her back and moved from the countertop, being careful not to take a step closer to him. Her reaction to him had unnerved her. She didn't know that she could trust herself not to reach out to him if she got too near.

'That's right,' he said. 'But I'm bored with all the physiotherapy and "taking it easy". I've been helping Ben and Sandy finish off the café.' He looked around him with a proprietorial air that she found disconcerting. 'Impressive, isn't it?'

'Very,' she said. 'I love the dolphin carvings. Every business in this town has to display some kind of dolphin motif, if I remember correctly. These are works of art.'

She kept her tone neutral but inside she was seething. In all their phone calls and Skype discussions about the progress of the café, Sandy had never once mentioned that Jesse was back in town. Her sister, along with everyone else in this gossip-ridden small town, knew she and Jesse had been caught making out on the balcony.

It wouldn't have been a huge deal anywhere else but here it was big news. Jesse was the kind of guy the locals kept odds on. The big bets were on that he would never settle down with one woman.

She found herself nervously glancing out of the plate glass windows that led to the street for fear people walking by might notice her and Jesse alone together.

She didn't want to become part of the Jesse mythology. Be a butt of local jokes. But her indiscretion on the night of the wedding meant, most likely, she'd been added to the list of his conquests. Why hadn't Sandy warned her Jesse had made an unscheduled visit home? That he'd be working on the café? It would be almost impossible to avoid him.

As Jesse reached out to touch the dolphin carvings, she jerked away from him to avoid any possible contact. He raised a dark eyebrow but didn't say anything. Which made her feel even more ill at ease.

'They're by the same Balinese carvers as the fittings next door in Bay Books,' he said, stroking the dolphin. She couldn't look, couldn't let herself remember how good his hands had felt on the bare skin of her back in her strapless bridesmaid dress. 'Sandy had the countertop custom-made and then imported it. I only finished installing it yesterday.'

'So you've completed work on the fit-out now?' She spoke through gritted teeth. *Please, please, please let him be on his way back to his job in the Philippines.*

'Just about.'

She sighed with too-obvious relief. 'So you won't be around much longer.'

Only a tightening of his beautifully chiselled lips betrayed he'd noticed her tone.

'There's the unpacking to do. And I still have to finish off some tiling upstairs in your apartment,' he said.

'You've been working up there?' She regretted the squawk of alarm as soon as it had escaped from her mouth. Jesse in her bathroom; maybe in her bedroom? The thought was disconcerting, to say the least.

But she couldn't let him know she was worried he would invade her private thoughts when she was alone in those rooms. *She mustn't let that happen*.

'Sandy wanted the bathroom remodelled to be as comfortable as possible for you and your little girl,' he said.

'Thank you for your help,' she managed politely. 'It was a big order to get it ready in time for us to move in.'

Her real gratitude was to Sandy. How many other down-on-their-luck chefs had a sister who had offered not only a job but also a place to live, rent-free?

But having Jesse Morgan around hadn't been part of the deal. She didn't want to be reminded of her lack of judgement on the night of the wedding. Of the folly of being in his arms. She should have known better than to fall for that kind of guy again.

Because, no matter how many times over the last six months she'd told herself that Jesse was bad news, seeing him again made her aware she'd be lying if she thought she was immune to him. He was still out-and-out the most attractive man she'd ever met. She would have to fight that attraction every moment she found herself in his company. Dear heaven, let there not be too many of those moments.

She looked purposefully around her again. 'I'd hate for the building work here to delay your recuperation.'

Jesse's deep blue eyes narrowed. 'So I can get the hell out of Dolphin Bay, you mean?'

She struggled to meet his gaze. 'I…I didn't mean it like that,' she lied.

His face set in grim lines. 'You might not like it but you'd better get used to me being around. I'm going to be here for at least another month while my shoulder heals.'

She couldn't help her little gasp of horror. 'What?'

Only the twist of his mouth indicated he'd heard. 'Sandy needs help to get this venture up and running and I intend to give it to her. The

Morgan family is grateful to Sandy. Heaven knows where Ben would be if she hadn't come back into his life after all those years.'

'Of course,' she said, suddenly feeling shamefaced that all she was thinking about was herself.

Lizzie and Sandy had first visited Dolphin Bay on a family vacation as teenagers. They'd stayed in the Morgan family's character-filled old guest house. Lizzie remembered Jesse from that time as an arrogant show-off, flexing his well-developed teenage muscles at any opportunity. But Sandy had fallen in love with Ben. They hadn't met again until twelve years later, after Ben had lost his first wife and baby son in the fire that had destroyed the guest house. Together they'd taken a second chance on love.

'I want to make this café a success for Sandy as well,' Lizzie continued. 'And for Ben, too—he's a marvellous brother-in-law. They've both been very good to me.'

Sandy was the only person she felt she could really trust. They'd been allies in the battleground that had been their family, led by their bully of a father. Her older sister had always watched out for her. Just like she was watching out for her and Amy now. Lizzie owed her.

'Then we're on the same page,' Jesse said.

'Right,' she said, unable to keep the anxiety from her voice.

'Bay Bites opens in a week's time. We don't have time to waste bickering,' Jesse said.

He took a few steps towards her until she was back up against that dolphin fin again and she couldn't back away from him any further. She felt breathless at his proximity, the memories of how good it had felt to be in his arms treacherously near the surface.

But this wasn't the fun, charming Jesse she'd known at the wedding bearing down on her. This Jesse looked tough, implacable and she didn't think it was her imagination that he seemed suddenly contemptuous of her.

'So better grit your teeth and bear being in my company for as long as it takes,' he said.

She'd had no idea his voice could sound so harsh.

CHAPTER TWO

JESSE NEARLY LAUGHED out loud at the expression of dismay on Lizzie's face. She so obviously didn't want to work with him any more than he wanted to work with her. Not after her behaviour at Ben and Sandy's wedding.

He could brush off his reputation as a player—but that wasn't to say he liked it. And he hadn't liked being made a fool of by Lizzie in the public arena of his brother's wedding reception. He hadn't appreciated having to make so many gritted teeth responses to his Dolphin Bay friends as they'd asked why Lizzie had left him high and dry when they'd so publicly been having a good time together. That had been difficult when he'd had no idea himself. There had been only so many jokes about whether he needed to change his deodorant that he could take. His banter had run dry long before he'd realised Lizzie wasn't coming back.

He indicated the packages propped up

against the wall. 'Right now I'm here to help you get those artworks up on the walls.'

'I'm not sure I need help,' she said, folding her arms in front of her. 'I'm quite capable of placing the artwork myself.'

Lizzie's looks were deceptive. Tall and slender with a mass of white blonde, finely curled hair, she gave the initial impression of being frail. But he knew there was steel under that fragile appearance. Her arms might be slim but they were firm with lean muscle. At the wedding she'd explained that hauling heavy cooking pans around a restaurant kitchen was a daily weight training regime.

'No,' he said curtly. 'That's my job and I'm here to do it.'

'What about your shoulder? Surely you shouldn't be lifting stuff.'

'Canvas artworks? Not a problem. This phase of my rehab calls for some light lifting.'

'But I need time to sort through them, to decide which paintings I like best.'

Her bottom lip stuck out stubbornly. She was putting up a fight. *Tough.* He'd promised Sandy he'd help out. For the years Ben had been immersed in grief, Jesse felt he had lost his adored older brother. Sandy's love had restored Ben to him. He could never thank her enough. If that meant having to spend too much time with her sister, he'd endure it. Lizzie could put up with it too.

He thought into the future and saw a long procession of family occasions where he and Lizzie would be forced into each other's company, whether they liked it or not. He had to learn to deal with it. So would she. And he would have to forever ignore how attractive he found her.

'That's where we read from the same page,' he said patiently, as if he were talking to a child. 'You choose. I hammer a nail in the wall and hang the picture. Then the artists want the rejects back ASAP.'

She looked startled. 'Rejects? I wouldn't want to offend any artists. Art appreciation is such a personal thing.'

'The artists have supplied these paintings to be sold on consignment,' he explained. 'You sell them through the café and get a commission on each sale. If they don't get hung this time, maybe they'll survive your cull next time.'

Lizzie nodded. It was the first time she'd agreed with him, though he sensed it took an effort. 'True. So I should probably compile an A-list for immediate hanging and a B-list for reserves. The Bs can then be ready to slip into place when the As are sold.'

'In theory a good idea. But keep the grading system to yourself. This is a small community.'

'Point taken,' she said, meeting his gaze square on. 'I'll defer to your small-town wisdom. We city people don't understand such things.'

He didn't miss the subtle edge of sarcasm to her words and again he had to fight a smile. He'd liked that tough core to her.

In fact when he'd met Lizzie at the pre-wedding party in Sydney for Ben and Sandy, he'd been immediately drawn to her. And not just for her good looks.

With her slender body, light blonde hair and cool grey eyes set in the pale oval of her face, she'd seemed ethereally lovely. But when she'd smiled, her eyes had lit up with a warmth and vivacity that had surprised him.

'Let's celebrate these long-lost lovers getting together in style,' she'd said with a big earthy laugh that had been a wholehearted invitation to fun. From then on, the evening had turned out a whole lot better than he'd expected.

Lizzie had made him laugh with her tales of life in the stressful, volatile world of commercial kitchens. That night had been memorable. So had the wedding reception a few days later. She'd kept him entertained with a game where she made amusing whispered predictions about the favourite foods of the other guests. All based on years of personal research into restaurant guests' tastes, she'd assured him with a straight face.

He hadn't been sure whether she was serious or not. Thing was, she'd been right more often than she'd been wrong. She'd had him watching the wedding guests as they made their choices at the buffet. He'd whooped with her when she'd got it right—his father heading straight for the fillet of beef—and commiserated with her when she'd got it wrong—an ultra-thin friend of the bride loading her plate with desserts. The game was silly, childish even, but he had thoroughly enjoyed every moment of her company. Those moments out on the balcony where she'd come so willingly into his arms had been a bonus.

At that time, he'd been in dire need of some levity and laughter, having just unexpectedly encountered the woman who had broken his heart years before. He'd first met the older, more worldly-wise Camilla when he'd been twenty-five; she'd been a photojournalist documenting his team's rebuilding of a flood-damaged community in Sri Lanka. He'd thought he'd never see her again after their disastrous break-up that had left him shattered and cynical about love, loyalty and trust.

At the wedding, lovely, spirited Lizzie had been both a distraction and a reminder that there could be life after treacherous Camilla.

Until Lizzie had walked out on him at the wedding without warning.

And now he was facing a completely different Lizzie. A Lizzie where it seemed as if the spark had fizzled right out of her. She was chilly. Standoffish. Hostile, even.

It made him wonder why he had found her appealing. He'd been so wrong about Camilla; seemed as if he'd misjudged Lizzie too.

He hadn't been on top of his game at that time; that was for sure.

And now, by the mere fact her sister was married to his brother, he was stuck with her. Trouble was, he still found her every bit as beautiful as when he'd first met her.

The sooner they got the paintings hung and the boxes unpacked, the sooner he could get out of here and away from her prickly presence. He'd endured some difficult situations in his time. But it looked as if putting up with Lizzie was going to be one of the most difficult of all. Even twenty minutes with her was stretching his patience. But there was work to be done and he'd made a commitment to Sandy.

He'd break his time working with Lizzie into

manageable blocks. He reckoned he could endure two hours of forced politeness in her company; manage to ignore how lovely she was. He'd make a strict schedule and stick to it. He looked at his watch. One hour and forty minutes to go. 'Let's get cracking on sorting those paintings. There's an amazing one of dolphins surfing I think you might want to look at first.'

Under her breath, Lizzie let off a string of curse words. She swore fluently in both English and French—it was difficult not to pick up some very colourful language working in the pressure cooker atmosphere of commercial kitchens.

But these days she kept a guard on her tongue. No way did she want Amy picking up any undesirable phrases. So she kept the curse words rolling only in her mind. This particular stream was directed—non-verbally of course—towards her sister. What had Sandy been thinking to trap her in such close confines with Jesse Morgan?

He was insufferable. Talking to her as if she was an idiot. Well, she had been an idiot to have fancied him so much at the wedding. To have let physical attraction overrule good sense. But that was then and this was now.

Like many chefs, during the years she had

worked in other peoples' restaurants, she had entertained the idea of running a restaurant of her own. In fact she and Philippe had been working towards just that until she'd unexpectedly fallen pregnant and everything had changed.

For sure, her dream of running her own show hadn't centred on a café in a place like Dolphin Bay but she could make the most of her downgraded dream. She knew what it took to make customers want to come to a restaurant—and to keep them coming. She didn't need Mr Know-It-All Jesse Morgan telling her how to choose the art for the walls. For heaven's sake, was he going to tell her what dishes to put on the menu?

She made a point of looking at her watch too. Two could play at this game. 'Okay, let's unwrap the paintings one at a time and then I'll compare them and decide which ones I like best. Without being so insensitive as to grade them, of course.'

For a moment she thought she saw a smile lurk around the corners of his grimly set mouth. It passed so quickly she could have imagined it. But for a second—just that second—she'd seen again that Jesse from the wedding who had appealed to her so much. Boy, had she got him wrong.

She walked across to the stacks of paintings. 'Shall we start with the largest one first?' she said.

Jesse nodded as he followed her over. 'That's the surfing dolphins one.'

She immediately wished she'd decided to open the smallest ones first. But she couldn't backtrack now.

The painting was bracketed with sheets of cardboard and then wrapped with thick brown paper. She started to open it but the paper was too tough to tear. Silently, Jesse reached into his pocket and pulled out a retractable-blade utility knife. Again without saying a word, he clicked it free of its safety cover and handed it to her.

'Thanks,' she muttered, biting down on the urge to tell him not to keep such a dangerous tool in his pocket. She knew she was being unreasonable, but Jesse seemed to have that effect on her. As much as she hated to admit it, she'd been hurt by his behaviour at the wedding, and she would do whatever it took to protect herself from feeling that way again.

She crouched down and carefully slit the paper across the top of the wrapping. As she went to cut down the side, Jesse reached out a hand to stop her.

She flinched. *Don't touch me*, she wanted

to snarl. But that would sound irrational. She gritted her teeth.

'Leave that,' he said. 'If you don't cut the sides the painting will be easier to get back in the wrapping.'

She stilled for the long moment his hand stayed on her wrist. Of course he had beautiful hands, just like the rest of him—she couldn't fail to register that. His fingers were warm and immediately familiar on her bare skin. She closed her eyes tight. *She couldn't deal with this.* But she was just about to shake off his hand when he removed it. She realised she was holding her breath and she let it out in a controlled sigh that she prayed he didn't register.

'Good idea,' she managed to choke out. *Why did he have to stand so close beside her?*

'I'll give you a hand to slide the painting out. It's too heavy for one person.'

She had to acknowledge the truth in that. It would seem churlish not to. 'Thanks,' she said.

She stood at one end of the painting and he at the other and they lifted it free of its wrappings. As the image emerged, she could not help a gasp. The artist had perfectly captured in acrylic, on the underside of a breaking aquamarine wave, a pod of dolphins joyfully surfing towards the beach. 'It's wonderful. No. More than wonderful. Breathtaking.'

Jesse would have been justified in an I-told-you-so smirk. Instead he nodded. 'I thought so too,' he said.

Lizzie reached out a hand to touch the painting then drew it back. 'This artist is so talented. It looks like Big Ray beach, is it?' Big Ray was the local surf beach. It had a different name on the maps. The locals called it Big Ray because of the two enormous dark manta rays that periodically glided their way from one headland to the other. As a kid, visiting Dolphin Bay, she had been both fascinated by and frightened of them.

'Yep. One of the smaller paintings is of the rays.'

'Let's open that one next.' She couldn't keep the excitement from her voice.

'So the big one passes muster?'

'Oh, yes,' she said. 'It gets a triple A. You were absolutely right. It's perfect.' She indicated a central spot on the wall. 'It would look fabulous right there.'

'I agree,' he said. 'The artist will be delighted. She was really hoping you'd choose one of her paintings.'

'*She?*' The word slipped out of her mouth.

Jesse's eyes darkened to the colour of the sea on a stormy day. 'Yes. She. Is that a problem?'

'Of course not. It's just—'

'It's just that you've jumped to the immediate wrong conclusion. The artist is a friend of my mother. A retired art teacher. I know her because she taught me at high school. Not because she's one of the infamous "Jesse's girls".'

'I...I didn't think that for one moment. Of course I didn't.' *Of course she had.*

At the wedding, she had wanted to be with Jesse so much, she had refused to acknowledge his reputation. Until he himself had shown her the truth of it.

She took a step away from him. His physical presence was so powerful she was uncomfortably aware of him. His muscular arms, tan against the white of his T-shirt. The strength of his chest. His flawless face. Stand too close and she could sense his body heat, breathe the spice of his scent that immediately evoked memories she was desperately trying to suppress.

She thought quickly. 'I...I just thought the artist might have been a man because of the sheer size and scale of the painting.'

'Fair enough,' he conceded, though to her eye he didn't look convinced. In fact she had the impression he was struggling to contain a retort. 'If you're sure you want this painting as the hero, let's get it up first so we can then balance the others around it.'

'That could work,' she said. He was right, of course he was right. And she could not let her memories of how he had hurt her hinder her from giving him the courtesy she owed him for his help.

He stood in front of the wall and narrowed his eyes. After a long pause he pointed. 'If we centre it there, I reckon we'll be able to achieve a balanced display.'

'Okay,' she said.

It wasn't a good idea to stand behind him. His rear view was even more appealing than she had remembered. Those broad shoulders, the butt that could sell a million pairs of jeans. She stepped forward so she was beside him. Darn, her shoulders were practically nudging his. Stand in front of him and she'd remember too well how he'd slid his arms around her and nuzzled her neck out on that balcony. *How she'd ached for so much more.* She settled for taking a few steps sidewards, so quickly she nearly tripped.

As it happened, she needn't have bothered with evasive tactics. He headed for a toolbox she hadn't noticed tucked away behind the counter and took out an electric drill, a hammer, a spirit level, a handful of plastic wall plugs and a jar of nails. 'It's a double brick wall with no electrics in the way so we can hang the picture exactly where we want it.'

'I can't wait to see it up,' she said.

She found his continual use of the word 'we' disconcerting. No way did she want to be thought as part of a team with Jesse Morgan. But, she had to admit, she was totally lacking in drilling skills. Sandy knew that. And why pay a handyman when Jesse was volunteering his time?

He pulled a pencil from out of his pocket, marked a spot on the wall and proceeded to drill. It seemed an awkward angle for someone with a shoulder injury but who was she to question him? But he easily drilled a neat hole, with only the finest spray of masonry dust to mar the freshly painted wall. 'Done,' he said in a satisfied tone.

He put down the drill, picked up the hammer and the wall plug. He positioned the wall plug with his left hand and took aim with the hammer in his right. His sudden curse curdled the air and the hammer thudded to the floor.

'Jesse! Are you okay?'

'Just my shoulder,' he groaned, gripping it and doubling over. 'Not a good angle for it.'

'How can I help?' She felt useless in the face of his pain. Disconcerted by her immediate urge to touch him, to comfort him.

He straightened up, wincing. 'You hold the nail and I'll wield the hammer using both hands, it'll take the strain off the shoulder.'

'Or you could let me use the hammer.'

'No,' he said. 'I'll do it.'

Was it masculine pride? Or did he honestly think she couldn't use a hammer? Whatever, she had no intention of getting into an argument over it. 'Okay,' she said.

He handed her the nail and, using her left hand, she positioned it against the wall plug. She was tall, but Jesse was taller. To reach the nail he had to manoeuvre himself around her. Her shoulders were pressed against the solid wall of his chest. *He was too close.* Her heart started to thud so fast she felt giddy; her knees went wobbly. She dropped the nail, twisted to get away from him and found herself staring directly up into his face. For a long, long moment their eyes connected.

'I…I can't do this, Jesse,' she finally stuttered as she pushed away from him.

Three of his large strides took him well away from her before he turned to face her again. He cleared his throat. 'You're right,' he said. 'We can't just continue to ignore what happened between us at the wedding. Or why you ran away the next day without saying goodbye.'

CHAPTER THREE

THE LIZZIE JESSE had known six months ago hadn't been short of a quick retort or a comment that bordered on the acerbic. Now she struggled to make a response. But he didn't prompt her. He'd waited six months for her excuse. He could wait minutes more.

Instead he tilted back on the heels of his boots, stuck his thumbs into the belt of his jeans and watched her, schooling his face to be free of expression.

She opened her mouth to speak then shut it again. She twisted a flyaway piece of her pale blonde hair that had worked itself free from the plait that fell between her shoulder blades.

'Not ignore. *Forget,*' she said at last.

'Forget us getting together ever happened?'

'Yes,' she said. 'It was a lapse of judgement on my part.'

He snorted. 'I've been insulted before but to be called a "lapse of judgement" is a first.'

She clapped her hand over her mouth. 'I didn't mean it to come out quite like that.'

'I'm tough; I can take it,' he said. He went to shrug his shoulders but it hurt. In spite of his bravado, so had her words.

'But I meant it,' she said. 'It should never have happened. The…the episode on the balcony was a mistake.' She had a soft, sweet mouth but her words twisted it into something bordering on bitter.

'I remember it as being a whole lot of fun,' he said slowly.

She tilted her chin in a movement that was surprisingly combative. 'Seems like our memories of that night are very different.'

'I remember lots of laughter and a warm, beautiful woman by my side,' he said.

By now she had braced herself against the back of the counter as if she wanted to push herself away from him as far as she possibly could. 'You mean you've forgotten the way a rowdy group of your friends came out and… and caught us—'

'Caught us kissing. Yeah. I remember. I've known those people all my life. They were teasing. You didn't seem to be bothered by it at the time.'

'It was embarrassing.'

'You were laughing.'

That piece of hair was getting a workout now between her slender fingers. 'To hide how I really felt.'

He paused. 'Do you often do that?'

She stilled. 'Laugh, you mean?'

He searched her face. 'Hide how you really feel.'

She met his gaze full on with a challenging tilt to her head. 'Doesn't everyone?'

'You laughed it off. Said you had to go check on Amy.'

Her gaze slid away so it didn't meet his. 'Yes.'

'You never came back.'

'I did but…but you were otherwise engaged.'

'Huh? I don't get it. I was waiting for you.' He'd checked his watch time and time again, but she still hadn't shown up. Finally he'd asked someone if they'd seen Lizzie. They'd pointed her out on the other side of the room in conversation with a group of the most gossipy girls in Dolphin Bay. She hadn't come near him again.

Now she met his eyes again, hers direct and shadowed with accusation. 'You were dancing with another woman. When you'd told me all dances for the evening were reserved for me.'

He remembered the running joke they had shared—Jesse with a 'Reserved for Lizzie' sign on his back, Lizzie with a 'Reserved for Jesse' sign. The possessiveness had been in jest but he had meant it.

He frowned. 'After the duty dances for the wedding—including with your delightful little daughter—the only woman I danced with that evening was you. Refresh my memory about the other one?'

She turned her head to the side. Her body language told him loud and clear she'd rather be anywhere else than here with him. In spite of the café and Sandy and family obligations.

'It was nothing,' she said, tight-lipped. 'You had every right to dance with another woman.'

He reached out and cupped her chin to pull her back to face him. 'Let's get this straight. I only wanted to dance with you that night.'

For a long moment he looked deep into her eyes until she tried to wiggle away from him and he released her. 'So describe this mystery woman to me,' he said.

'Black hair, tall, beautiful, wearing a red dress.' It sounded as if the words were being dragged out of her.

He frowned.

'You seemed *very* happy to be with her,' she prompted.

Realisation dawned. 'Red dress? It was my cousin. I was with my cousin Marie. She'd just told me she was pregnant. She and her husband had been trying for years to start a family. I was talking with her while I waited for you to come back.'

'Oh,' Lizzie said in a very small voice, her head bowed.

'I wasn't dancing with her. More like whirling her around in a dance of joy. A baby is everything she's always wanted.'

'I...I'm glad for her,' Lizzie said in an even more diminished voice.

He couldn't keep the edge of anger from his voice. 'You thought I'd moved on to someone else? That I'd kissed you out on the balcony—in front of an audience—and then found another woman while you were out of the room for ten minutes?'

She looked up at him. 'That's what it seemed like from where I was standing. I've never felt so foolish.'

'So why didn't you come over and slap me on the face or whack me with your purse or do whatever jealous women do in such circumstances?'

'I wasn't jealous. Just...disappointed.' Her gaze slid away again.

'I was disappointed when you didn't come back. When you took off to Sydney the next day without saying goodbye. When you didn't return my phone calls.'

'I…I…misunderstood. I'm sorry.'

She turned her back on him and walked around the countertop so it formed a physical barrier between them. When she got to the glass jars she picked one up and put it down. He noticed her hands weren't quite steady.

Even with the counter between them, it would be easy to lean over and touch her again. Even kiss her. He fought the impulse. She so obviously didn't want to be touched. And he didn't want to start anything he had no intention of continuing. He wanted to clear up a misunderstanding that had festered for six months. That was all. He took a step back to further increase the distance between them.

'I get what happened. You believed my bad publicity,' he said.

'Publicity? I don't know what you mean.' But the flickering of her eyelashes told him she probably had a fair idea of what he meant.

'My reputation. Don't tell me you weren't warned about me. That I'm a player. A ladies' man. That you'd be one of "Jesse's girls" until I tired of you.'

How he'd grown to hate that old song from the nineteen-eighties where the singer wailed over and over that he wanted 'Jessie's girl'. Apparently his parents had played it at his christening party and it had followed him ever since; had become his signature song.

She flushed high on her cheeks. 'No. Of course not.'

'You should know—reports of my love life are greatly exaggerated.'

He used to get a kick out of his reputation for being a guaranteed girl magnet—what freewheeling guy in his teens and early twenties wouldn't?—though he'd never taken it seriously. But now, as thirty loomed, he was well and truly over living up to the Jesse legend. A legend that had always been more urban myth than fact.

But he'd done nothing to dispel it. In fact it had been a convenient shield against ever having to explain why he'd closed his heart off against a committed relationship. Why he dated fun-for-now, unchallenging girls and always stayed in control of where the relationship went.

Camilla's words haunted him. *You won't miss me for a minute; a guy as good-looking as you can get any woman you want just by snapping your fingers—there'll always be another one waiting in line.* It wasn't true, as she herself had proven. He had wanted her. Badly. And she had gutted and filleted his heart as surely as his father did the fish he caught. He would never expose himself to that kind of pain again.

'I didn't need to be warned,' Lizzie said. 'I figured it out for myself. You and Kate Parker, Sandy's other bridesmaid, were the talk of the wedding. How you'd come back from your travels and hooked up with her. How Kate wouldn't have more luck with getting you to commit than any other of the long line of girl-friends before her.'

As he'd suspected, the Dolphin Bay gos-sips had struck again. Didn't the women in this town have anything better to do with their time? Though for all their poking their noses into other people's business, they'd never come close to ferreting out the reasons why he'd stayed so resolutely single.

Kate had been his childhood friend. There'd been a long-standing joke between their fami-lies that if they hadn't met anyone else by the time they were aged thirty they'd settle down with each other.

'Not true. We kissed. Once. To see if there was anything more than friendship between us. There wasn't. We were just friends. Still are friends.'

Lizzie shrugged. 'I realised that. I soon

sussed out she only had eyes for the other groomsman, your friend Sam Lancaster.'

'True. It seemed like one minute Kate was organising Ben and Sandy's wedding, the next minute she was planning her own.'

'I heard they eloped and got married at some fabulous Indian palace hotel.'

'You heard right. I was Sam's best man. It turned out great for them,' he said.

He was really happy for his old friends. But if he was honest with himself, there had been an awkward moment when Kate had made it very clear the kiss had been a disaster for her. Coming on top of what had happened with Camilla it had struck a serious blow to his male pride. By the time of the wedding he'd been in a real funk, questioning things about himself he'd never before had cause to question.

Meeting Lizzie had done a lot to help soothe his bruised ego—until she'd walked away without a word of explanation.

But that had been six months ago. He'd moved on. Now his circumstances were very different. He'd come to a real turning point in his career and the path he chose was crucial to his future. The recent encounter with Camilla had made him realise it could be time to move on from his work with the charity. He'd told his boss there was a good chance he wouldn't return after his shoulder healed. He would not turn his back on it completely but would remain involved as a volunteer and as a fund-raiser.

A new direction had opened with the offer of a fast-track job with a multinational construction company based in Houston, Texas. It would be a challenging, demanding role in a ruthlessly competitive commercial environment. But living in the United States would mean he'd rarely make it home to Dolphin Bay.

As far as Lizzie went, he just wanted to clear up a misunderstanding that had left her resentful of him and him disappointed in her. They'd missed their chance to be any kind of couple, even the most casual. Once the misunderstanding was sorted, they could work together without awkwardness. After all, she was part of the family now and would always be around. They had to come to some sort of mutual good terms.

'Weddings have a lot to answer for,' she said. 'All that romance and emotion floating around makes people do things they really shouldn't. Fool around when they shouldn't. Behave in ways they later regret.'

'Just for the record, I wasn't just fooling around with you at the wedding,' he said.

She flushed redder. 'Maybe I was just fooling around with you.'

'Maybe you were.'

'Maybe *I'm* the player,' she said. There was a return of that teasing spirit he'd liked so much, a spark that warmed her cool grey eyes. He found himself wanting her to smile.

Jesse only vaguely remembered Lizzie from her first visit to Dolphin Bay. She'd been sixteen, beanpole-thin and flat-chested. He'd been sixteen, too. But testosterone had well and truly kicked in and he'd considered himself a man.

He wasn't ashamed to admit he hadn't found her attractive then. He'd been a typical teenage boy who'd looked to the more obvious.

That summer, his brother Ben had been busy falling in love with Sandy. Jesse had been busy trying to decide between three curvaceous older girls who'd made their interest in him more than clear. He hadn't chosen any of them. Even then he hadn't valued what came to him too easily.

When he'd met Lizzie again, more than twelve years later, he'd been knocked over at the woman she'd become. Elegant; sensual without being blatantly sexy; classy. Now she wore simple narrow-legged jeans and a plain white shirt with the sleeves rolled up. Her hair was tied back off her face in a plait. She looked sensational without even trying.

'Are you a player?' he asked. 'I somehow doubt that.'

Her eyes dimmed and it was as if that hint of party-girl Lizzie had been extinguished again. 'No. I'm a divorced single mum with a social life on hold indefinitely. I'm here to work hard at making this café a success and to devote myself to Amy.'

'I get that,' he said. 'Being a lone parent must be one of the toughest gigs around.'

'Tougher than I could have imagined,' she said. 'But it's worth it. Amy is the best thing that ever happened to me.'

'You were young when you had her.'

'Becoming a mother at age twenty-three wasn't part of my game plan, I can assure you. But I don't regret it even for a second.'

He frowned. 'Where is Amy? Didn't she drive down with you from Sydney?'

Lizzie's daughter was a cute kid; she'd been the flower girl at the wedding and charmed everyone. He'd been sorry he hadn't had the chance to say goodbye to her too.

'She's spending the school vacation in France with her father and his parents. They love her and want her to grow up French. That's another reason I have to make a success of this café. Philippe would like sole custody and is just waiting for me to fail.'

Sandy had told Jesse a bit of Lizzie's background. The domineering father. The early marriage. The break-up with the French husband. She hadn't had it easy. Just as well nothing more had happened with them at the wedding. He wouldn't want to have added to her burden of hurt. He knew what that felt like.

'You'll have a lot of support here,' he said. 'Sandy's a Morgan now and the Morgans look after their own.'

'I know that. And I'm grateful. But I'll still have to work, work, work.' She took a deep breath, looked directly up at him. 'I'm truly sorry I misread the situation with your cousin. But what happened between us at the wedding can't happen again; you know that, don't you?'

Relief flooded through him that she had no expectations of him. She was lovely, quite possibly the loveliest woman he knew. But right now he didn't want to date anyone either. Not seriously. And Lizzie was the type of person who would expect serious.

'Lizzie, I—' he started, but she spoke over him.

'I told you my social life is on hold. That means no dating. Not you. Not anyone.'

'I get that,' he said.

His life was so far removed from Lizzie's. His job took him to all the points of the earth for extended periods of time. If he ever committed to a woman it would have to be someone without ties. Camilla would have been ideal—a freelance photojournalist with no kids, feisty, independent. But what had happened with Camilla had soured him against getting close to her type of woman.

'Good,' Lizzie said, rather more vehemently than his ego would have liked.

'I hope you can remember what we had at the wedding as no-strings fun that I certainly don't regret,' he said.

She nodded. He didn't know whether he should be insulted, the way she was so eager to agree.

'But it—' he started to say.

'Can't happen again,' she joined in so they chorused the words.

He extended his hand to her over the counter. 'Friends?'

She hesitated and didn't take his hand. 'I'm not sure about "friends"—we hardly know each other. I don't call someone a friend lightly.'

He resisted the urge to roll his eyes. 'Yep.'

Her eyes widened at his abrupt reply. 'I don't mean to be rude,' she said. 'Just honest about what I feel.'

Yeah. She was. But her honesty had a sharp edge. All in all, it made him wonder why he'd want to be friends with her anyway. Especially when he knew she was off-limits to anything more than friendship. It would be difficult to be 'just friends' with someone he found so attractive. That two-hour limit he'd set himself on the time he spent with her might just be two hours too much.

'So "just acquaintances" or "just strangers stuck with each other's company" might be more to the point?' he said.

She gasped. 'That sounds dreadful, doesn't it?' Then she disarmed him with a smile—the kind of open, appealing smile that had drawn him to her in the first place. 'Too honest, even for me. After all, we can *try* to be friends, can't we?'

'We can try to be friends,' he agreed. *Two hours at a time.* Any more time than that with her each day and he might find himself wanting more than either of them was prepared to give. And that was dangerous.

'Okay,' she said, this time taking his hand in hers in a firm grip, shaking it and letting it go after the minimum contact required to seal the deal.

CHAPTER FOUR

LIZZIE LEANED BACK from the last of the art-works they'd rewrapped to send back to the artist, kneading with fisted hands the small of her back where it ached. 'That's it,' she said. 'All done, thank goodness. That was harder work than I'd thought it would be.'

'But worth it,' said Jesse from beside her.

'Absolutely worth it. The paintings add to the atmosphere of the café like nothing else could. I hope the artists come in so I can thank them with a coffee.'

But Lizzie felt exhausted. Not just from the effort of unpacking, holding the paintings up against the wall and then repacking the un-wanted pictures. But from the strain of work-ing alongside Jesse.

In theory, learning to be 'just friends' with him should have been easy. He was personable, smart, and seemed determined to put their his-tory behind them. Gentlemanly, too—in spite of his shoulder injury he insisted on doing any heavy lifting.

Trouble was, she found it impossible to relax around him. She had to consider every word before she uttered it, which made her sound stilted and awkward. The odd uncharacteristic nervous giggle kept bubbling into her conversation.

Could you ever be just friends with a man you'd kissed, wanted, cried over? Especially when that man was so heart-stoppingly attractive. *Could you pretend that time together had never happened?*

She would have to try.

If it were up to her, she would choose never to see Jesse Morgan again. Even though they'd cleared up the misunderstanding about his cousin, it was hard to be around someone she'd fancied, kissed, liked…when nothing would—or could—ever happen between them. But with the family situation being the way it was, she had to make a real effort to nurture a friendship with him—be pals, buddies, good mates. Future family occasions could be incredibly awkward if she didn't.

Right now, Jesse stood beside her as they both surveyed the arrangement of paintings on the wall. He was not so close that their shoulders were in danger of nudging but close enough so she was aware of his scent, an intoxicating blend of spicy sandalwood and fresh male sweat. It was *too* close. Being anywhere within touching distance of Jesse Morgan was too close. Memories of how wonderful it had felt to be in his arms were resurfacing.

She leaned forward to straighten the small painting of the manta rays and used the movement to edge away, hoping he didn't notice.

'They look good,' Jesse said. 'You chose well.'

She thought about a friend-type thing to say. 'To be fair, we both made the final selection.'

'You exercised your power of veto more often than not.'

'Is that another way of saying I'm a control freak?' she said without thinking at all.

'I didn't say that,' he said, a smile lurking at the corners of his mouth. 'But…'

If he was a real friend, she would have punched him lightly on the arm for that and laughed. She wished it could be that way. But there would be no casual jesting and certainly no touching with Jesse. It was too much of a risk.

Instead she made a show of sighing. 'The success or failure of Bay Bites rests on my shoulders and I'm only too aware of that.'

'That's not true,' he said. 'You do have help. Sandy. Ben. The staff she's hired for you. Me.'

She turned to face him. 'You?'

'I can work with you for two hours a day.'

'Two hours?' That seemed an arbitrary amount of time to allocate. Maybe it was all he could manage with his shoulder. But she couldn't help wondering what other commitments Jesse had in Dolphin Bay. And if they were of the female kind.

He nodded. 'Whatever help you need, I'm there for two hours every day.'

That was the trouble with denying attraction when that attraction was an ever-present tension, underlying every word, every glance. The air seemed thick with words better left unspoken. At a different time, in a different life, she could think of some exciting ways to spend two hours alone with Jesse Morgan in her bedroom. *But not now.*

She cleared her throat. *Think neutral, friend-type chat.* 'I appreciate the help with the paintings. Though I'm the one who will be looking at them all day and—call me a control freak—but I really couldn't say yes to the one of the bronze whaler sharks, no matter how skilfully it was done.'

He'd argued hard for the sharks and he continued to argue. 'Sharks are part of the ocean.

As a surfer I learned to respect them. They're magnificent creatures. That painting captured them perfectly.'

She shuddered. 'They're predators. And I don't like predators. Also, remember people will be eating in this place. They don't want to look up and see pictures of creatures that might eat *them.*'

Jesse grinned, his perfect teeth white against his tan, those blue, blue eyes glinting with good humour. *A woman could forget all caution and common sense to win a smile like that.*

Again she found herself wishing things could be different, that they could take up from where they'd left off out on that balcony. She had to suppress a sigh at the memory of how exciting his kisses had been.

'Good point,' he said. 'But I still think there are too many wussy pictures of flowers.'

'So we agree to disagree,' she said with an upward tilt of her chin.

'Wussy versus brave?' he challenged, still with that grin hovering on his so-sexy mouth.

'If by brave you mean you want to swim with the sharks, then go for it. I'll stick with dolphins, thanks.'

'I've always liked a challenge,' he said.

The challenge of the chase? Was that what he meant? Lizzie really didn't want to know.

Or to think too much about how it would feel
to be caught up again in Jesse's arms. She'd
just steer clear of him as much as she could.
It wasn't that she didn't trust him not to over-
step the boundaries of a new friendship—it
was herself she didn't trust.

'I do love the painting of the dolphins surfing,' she said. 'If I could afford the price tag,
I'd buy it myself.'

He sobered. 'You'll have to make sure you
don't get too attached to any of the paintings.
You want to sell as many as you can. It's an
added revenue stream for the café.'

'You're right. I'll just get heartbroken when
that particular one goes.'

'Just think of the commission on the sale,'
he said. 'The quicker the café gets in the black,
the better it will be for all concerned.'

She was surprised at how hard-headed and
businesslike he sounded. But of course Jesse
would be used to not getting attached to pretty
things. And that was when she had to bite
down on any smart remarks. Not if they were
going to try to be friends.

'Thanks again for your help,' she said. 'I'd
offer you some lunch but, as you can see, I'm
not set up for food just yet.'

'I hear you're still finalising the menu. I'm

looking forward to being an official food taster on Saturday.'

Lizzie stared. 'You're coming to the taste test?'

'Sandy rounded up all the family to help you try out the recipes.'

'Oh,' she said, disconcerted. If she'd thought she'd only be seeing Jesse occasionally during his time back home in Dolphin Bay, she was obviously mistaken. Talking herself out of her attraction to him was going to get even more difficult.

'When it comes to taste-testing good food, I'm your man,' he said.

She remembered the game they'd had such fun playing together at the wedding, predicting the favourite foods of the guests. He'd been such good company she'd forgotten all the worries that plagued her that night. *Good company and something more that had had her aching for him to kiss her out on that balcony.*

'Let me guess,' she said, resting her chin on her hand, making a play of thinking hard. 'The other volunteers will have to fight you for the slow-roasted lamb with beetroot relish. And maybe the caramelised apple pie with vanilla bean ice cream?'

He folded his arms in front of his chest. 'I'm not going to tell you if you're right or wrong about what I like. You'll have to wait for the taste night to see.'

'Tease,' she said.

'You don't like being made to wait, do you?' he said, that slow smile still playing at the corners of his mouth.

'There are some things that are worth waiting for,' she said, unable to resist a slow smile of her own in return.

For a long moment her eyes met his until she dropped her gaze. *She had to stop this*. It would be only too easy to flirt with Jesse, to fall back into his arms and that way could lead to disaster. She had to keep their conversations purely on a business level.

She glanced through the connecting doorway and into the bookshop. Sandy was due to see her at any time and there was only a small moment of opportunity left with Jesse.

She lowered her voice. 'Can I ask you something in confidence?'

His dark brows rose. 'Sure. Ask away.'

'I'm concerned about the food I've got to work with.'

'Concerned?'

'It…it might not be up to scratch.'

He frowned. 'I'm not sure what you mean. Aren't the food supplies being ordered through the Hotel Harbourside restaurant? Ben's hotel is one of the best places to eat in town.'

Ben had built the modern hotel on the site of the old guest house. Alongside, he'd built a row of shops, including Bay Books and Bay Bites.

She winced at Jesse's understandably defensive tone. But who else could she ask? 'That's the problem. I have to tread carefully. But I have to be blunt. The Harbourside is good pub grub. Nothing more. Nothing less. And it's not up to the standard I want. Not for Bay Bites.'

Lizzie did tend to be blunt. Jesse had noticed that six months ago. Personally, he appreciated her straightforward manner. But not everyone in Dolphin Bay would. No way could the café succeed if Lizzie was going to look down her straight, narrow little nose at the locals. Could she really fit in here?

'But isn't it just a café?' he said.

'*Just* a café? How can you say that?' Her voice rose with indignation. 'Because it's a café doesn't mean it can't serve the best food I can possibly offer. Whether I'm cooking in a high-end restaurant or a café, my food will be the best.' She gave a proud toss to her head that he doubted she even realised she'd made.

There was a passion and an energy to her that he couldn't help but admire. But he also feared for her. Small country towns could be brutal on newcomers they thought were too big for their boots.

'You're not in France now, Lizzie.'

'More small town wisdom for me?' Her half-smile took the snarkiness out of the comment.

'Some advice—you don't want to make things too fancy. Not a good idea around here to give the impression you think everything is better in France. Or in Sydney.'

Her response was somewhere between a laugh and a snort. 'You seriously think I'm going to transplant fancy French dining to a south coast café and expect it to work? I might have lived in France for years, but I'm still an Aussie girl and I think I've got a good idea of what my customers will like.'

He knew she had a reputation as a talented chef who had established her credentials at a very young age—he wasn't sure she had the business sense to go with them.

'And that would be?' he asked.

'The very best ingredients served simply.' She gave another toss of her head that sent her blonde plait swishing across her back. 'That's what I learned in France. Not necessarily at the fine-dining establishments in Paris but in the cafés and markets of Lyon and from the home cooking of Amy's French grandparents. You know they say the heart of France is Paris, but its stomach is Lyon?'

'I didn't know that.' He'd raced through a see-Europe-in-two-weeks type backpacker tour when he was a student that had included Paris and Versailles but that was as far as his knowledge of the country went. 'My journeys have mainly been of the have-disaster-will-travel type. And the food…well, you wouldn't want to know about the food.'

'Of course,' she said, nodding. 'I remember now you told me about some of the out-of-the-way places you've been sent to.'

She'd seemed so genuinely interested in the work he was doing to rebuild communities. Not once had she voiced concern that he had veered off the career track to big bucks and business success. Other girls had been more vocal. He hadn't seen the need to explain to them that he'd been fortunate in the land he'd inherited from his grandparents and the investments he'd made. He could afford to work for a charity for as long as it suited him and not have to justify it to anyone.

Though that might be about to change. The Houston company wanted his expertise and their offer came with a salary that had stunned him with the amount of zeroes.

'So what's your problem with ordering through the hotel?' he asked.

'Their suppliers will be fine for the basics and the hotel gives us better buying power. It's the organic and artisan produce I worked with in Sydney I need to source. Farm to plate stuff. I don't know where to get it here.'

'Farm to plate? That sounds expensive. Do you really want expensive for the café?' He looked around at the fresh white décor, the round tables and bentwood chairs, the way the layout had been designed for customers to wander in from the bookshop. It said casual and relaxed to him.

'Actually, farm to plate can be less expensive because you cut out the middle man.'

'That's a point,' he said.

'I know ridiculously high prices would be the kiss of death to a café serving breakfast and lunch,' she said with that combative tilt to her chin that was starting to get familiar in an endearing kind of way.

'It's good we agree on that one,' he said.

'But if Bay Bites is to succeed it has to be so much better than the existing cafés around here. What would you prefer—a cheap burger made with a mass-produced beef patty or pay a dollar or two extra for free-range, hand-ground beef? Frozen fries or hand cut fries with home-made mayo?'

'That's a no-brainer,' he said, his stomach becoming aware it was lunchtime and rumbling at the thought of the burger. Though the slow-roasted lamb might give it some competition. 'So you are talking café food, not fancy-schmantzy stuff?'

'Of course I am,' she said, not hiding her exasperation. 'I know people will expect the basics.'

'Egg and bacon roll?' he said hopefully.

'The best you've ever tasted. But there will be some more creative options too, depending on seasonal ingredients. And wonderful desserts every day, of course. We'll do morning and afternoon tea as well as breakfast and lunch.'

'You mentioned apple pie?' The longing crept into his voice, in spite of himself.

She nodded with a knowing smile. He'd given himself away. There was no dessert he liked better than apple pie. She'd guessed right again.

'What I'm asking you is how I source that produce without offending Sandy and Ben,' she said.

'How long is it since you've spent any time in Dolphin Bay?'

'There was the wedding. And I drove down to see the building when Sandy first approached me about the café.'

'So basically your memories of the food here are based on when you were sixteen?' Back when there'd been a fish and chip shop, a short-lived pizza place and the best food in town had been from his mother's kitchen.

'Well, yes.'

'Better get yourself up to date. This area has become somewhat of a foodie haven.'

'Dolphin Bay?' Disbelief underscored her words.

'Maybe not the actual town,' he conceded. 'But certainly the areas surrounding it. Didn't you look into that when you did your business plan?'

She pulled a face that made him want to smile but she was so serious he kept his expression neutral.

'Sandy and Ben did the business plan,' she said. 'And they're dead certain there's a market for a bookshop café with a harbour view. But I had to finish a work contract in Sydney and didn't have time to do as much research into the local area as I would have liked.'

'If you had, you would have found one of the well-known television chefs opened a restaurant in the next town and others have followed. Every time I come home on leave, there seem to be more restaurants.'

Her fine eyebrows rose in surprise. 'That's good. Hopefully the rising tide will float all our boats. But where are they sourcing the artisan produce? And how do I get it without offending my sister?'

Did he want to get this involved with this woman, helping her beyond what he'd agreed to with Sandy when he'd volunteered to give a hand while he was on leave? He knew the answer before he'd even finished asking himself the question.

He'd promised Sandy to do his best to make the café succeed. If that meant getting Lizzie what she wanted, he didn't have a choice. And it had nothing to do with how lovely she was, he told himself. Or how intriguing he found her.

'Ben and I grew up with people who have established organic farms and orchards in the area, if that's what you're looking for. And the seafood comes fresh from our own father's boats.'

'Really?' Her cool grey eyes lit up. 'Sandy told me about the seafood. But I didn't know about the organic farms.'

He tilted back on his boot heels again and

stuck his thumbs in his belt. 'I suspect all you need is here if you know where to look for it.'

'Trouble is, I don't.' She tilted her head to the side as she looked at him and smiled very sweetly.

Jesse suppressed a groan. He knew what was coming. 'You're going to ask me to introduce you to those places, aren't you?'

'Of course I am.' Again he was struck by how a smile brought such light to her face. She'd been so warm and vivacious at the wedding that he'd found it hard to leave her side for even a minute.

'Okaaay…' He drew out the word in mock reluctance. 'I guess I can do that for you.'

It wouldn't be a hardship to show her around, if he kept his distance from anything too personal. *Trying to be friends—that was all*. It would also be a chance to catch up with people he hadn't seen for ages. His job meant he'd lost touch with more friends from the area than he'd like.

'Does that count in your daily two hours of rationed help?' she asked.

His immediate impulse was to say *of course not*. But then he thought twice.

On meeting Lizzie again, he'd thought he'd only be able to endure two hours of her chilly, stand-offish company. Now the Lizzie he'd first fallen for was starting to reveal herself. Warm. Funny. With a touch of snark that challenged him. He didn't want his initial attraction to her to be reignited. That meant seeing as little of her as possible. Now that two-hour limit would be not because he didn't like her— rather because he didn't want to get to like her too much.

Lizzie could never be a casual encounter. An *it's been nice but I don't want to get serious* type of thing. No. Anything with Lizzie would be serious with a capital S. She was a mother with a child, making the relationship equation two-plus-one, rather than the one-plus-one he was used to. She was also his brother's sister-in-law. If they started something and it broke up, the repercussions would be endless.

There were many reasons to steer clear—not least that he saw in her the same kind of spirited, challenging personality that had drawn him to Camilla with such disastrous results. His life was on track with the prospect of a new start in America. He didn't want any awkward emotional confrontations to derail him if he again fell for the wrong woman.

Six months ago he'd been very taken with Lizzie, had seen the possibility of something more than a casual hook-up at a wedding. Looking back, he could see he'd been raw from his recent encounter with Camilla. Lovely Lizzie's laughter and passionate kisses had been affirmation of his appeal as a man, balm to his shattered heart and bruised ego. But her inexplicable cold treatment of him had plunged him back into his resolve to stay clear of women with the power to wound him.

Now this job offer had further strengthened his resolve to avoid anything remotely connected to commitment to a woman. He needed to remain unencumbered if he were to move up to this new stage in his career. The CEO of the Houston company had pretty much spelled out it was a job for a single man—travelling, lots of overtime and weekend work.

That two-hour restriction on time with Lizzie would stay—he couldn't let himself get to like her too much. He genuinely wanted to try and become friends, though. After all, she'd be part of his life for as long as her sister was married to his brother and that looked likely to be for ever. Two hours a day was more than enough to develop the kind of superficial friendship that didn't make any demands on him—or, in fact, on her. He couldn't deny his attraction to Lizzie—but he could stop himself from acting on it.

'Yes, two hours is all I can spare,' he said.

'None of the farms we'll be going to is far from here.'

He could tell she was perplexed by the time restriction but he had no intention of explaining it to her.

'Okay,' she said. Starting tomorrow, please. I don't have time to waste.'

Lizzie was grateful that Jesse was able to help her with her dilemma. She was about to tell him so when Sandy swept into the shop, all exclamations of delight at how the café was shaping up.

Lizzie silently implored Jesse with her eyes to please not say anything of their conversation about the supplies. Thankfully, he indicated with a slight incline of his head that he would keep her confidence. Not in a million years would she want to cause offence to Sandy or Ben. At the same time, she had to have the best for the café.

Brown-haired, hazel-eyed Sandy swept her into a big hug and she squeezed her sister back hard. The wonderful thing about being in Dolphin Bay was it meant more time with her.

'I am *so* glad you got here okay,' Sandy said. She then looked to Jesse. 'I'm still pinching myself that I got a chef of my sister's calibre to run Bay Bites for us. Aren't we fortunate?'

'We're very lucky,' he agreed.

Sandy hugged Jesse, too, and it gave Lizzie pleasure to see the depth of affection between her sister and her brother-in-law.

She and Sandy had both been so emotionally damaged by their controlling cheater of a father that for a while it had looked as if neither of them would find happiness with a man. But Sandy was now blissfully married to Ben and had been lovingly welcomed into the close-knit Morgan family.

One out of two sisters sorted with a happy-ever-after wasn't bad, Lizzie thought. Philippe had done such a good job of destroying any trust she'd had left in men she doubted there'd ever be a second chance of happiness for her. And certainly not if she kept getting attracted to gorgeous love-'em-and-leave-'em guys like Jesse. She didn't regret kissing him at the wedding. Could never forget how wonderful her time with him had been. But it would never happen again.

'I'm so glad to be here,' she said to Sandy. 'It's the new start I need.'

'I see you two have reacquainted yourselves,' Sandy said, waving to Jesse.

With an emphasis on *acquaintance* Lizzie wanted to say, but knew it would come out sounding ill-mannered.

'Yes,' she murmured, avoiding Jesse's gaze. He just nodded.

Lizzie did not fail to detect the speculation in her sister's eyes as Sandy looked from her to Jesse and back again.

Guess she'd better get used to seeing that look in other people's eyes, too, when they saw her and Jesse together—until it became obvious the incident at the wedding was all there ever was going to be between them.

Sandy spun around to the wall behind her. 'The paintings look amazing the way you've hung them.'

'I have to give credit where credit is due,' said Lizzie, indicating Jesse with a sweep of her hand. 'He put them all up.'

'The boss is the one who chose them,' said Jesse.

'The boss?' asked Lizzie.

'That's you,' he said. 'I jump to your command.' His words were light-hearted but his already deep voice dropped an octave or two as he spoke.

She had to disguise her gasp of awareness with a cough. Oh, she could think of lots of commands she could give to beautiful Jesse, alone and behind closed doors. But not when they were 'just friends'. Not when he was her sister's brother-in-law. Not when he was a man who had a reputation for toying with women's hearts.

She was spared making any kind of smart reply by Jesse himself. He glanced at his watch. 'I didn't realise it was that late. Gotta go.'

'Your two hours are up?' she said, still intrigued by the limit he had given her on his time.

'What two hours?' asked Sandy.

'Something to do with his shoulder,' said Lizzie.

'Yeah, my shoulder, that's it,' said Jesse gruffly. 'I'll pick you up at ten tomorrow,' he said to Lizzie. 'Bye, Sandy.'

Lizzie watched in silent admiration as Jesse strode out of Bay Bites with a masculine loping grace. His back view really was something to see. Broad shoulders tapered to a tight behind. Worn denim jeans hugged muscular legs. And those tanned brown arms rippled with muscle. If he were any other gorgeous guy than Jesse Morgan she'd want to give him a wolf whistle. 'No!' said her sister, once Jesse was out of earshot.

'What do you mean "no"?'

'I saw the way you were looking at Jesse.'

'And you weren't too?'

'Of course I wasn't,' Sandy said primly. 'He's my brother-in-law.'

'And that doesn't stop you appreciating what a finely crafted specimen of masculinity he is?'

'Of course it does,' Sandy said. 'I'm a married woman.' But then the giggles she was suppressing pealed out. 'I wouldn't be female if I didn't appreciate how hot Jesse is. And he's a nice guy too. But he's a commitment-phobe of the first order.'

'I know, I know. If you told me once you told me a million times.'

'And at the wedding you totally ignored my warnings.'

'That was different. Cut me a break, Sandy. I was lonely. Starved for male company. Heck, starved for adult company outside of a commercial kitchen. And Jesse was…was irresistible.'

Lizzie swallowed hard against a hitch in her voice when she remembered the magic of those hours with Jesse. It hadn't been just physical— for her, anyway. At the wedding she'd seen a spark of 'what might have been' if circumstances had been different.

'I love Jesse to pieces. But I don't want to see you hurt.' Sandy paused. 'Or, for that matter, see Jesse hurt.'

'What do you mean, "see Jesse hurt"?'

'Were you serious about him at the wedding? Or was he just a fling before you got back to the reality of being a single mum?'

'Of course I wasn't serious—how could I be with all those warnings echoing in my head?' *Though there had been moments when she'd been guilty of daydreaming of something more.* 'Jesse was fun. A diversion. He made me laugh at a time when I didn't have a whole lot to laugh about.'

'That's what I mean. We'd be angry if a guy toyed with a pretty woman just for a diversion. Why would it be different for a woman with a handsome guy?'

'You can't be serious. I wasn't *toying* with Jesse. It's not the same thing at all.'

'Isn't it? Seems to me there's a lot more to Jesse than he lets on. Sometimes I think it might be a disadvantage to be as good-looking as he is. Does he ever wonder if women flock to him because of how he looks or because of who he is?'

'It's not something I've thought about,' Lizzie said.

'People think women are throwing themselves at him all the time and he wouldn't care if someone dumped him like you did. He was gutted when you went home without another word to him, though he tried to hide it.'

'R-really?' was all Lizzie could manage to

stutter. Could that be true? She'd only thought of her own hurt feelings. 'There…there was a misunderstanding. But we've sorted that out. It's been six months. I…I'm sure there've been other women for him in the meantime.'

It was ridiculous, but her heart twisted painfully at the thought of Jesse with someone else. Even now, when she'd put him strictly off-limits.

She'd been stabbed by a sharp and unexpected shard of jealousy when she'd rushed back to the wedding reception to find Jesse with the woman she now knew was his cousin. Her jealousy had been disproportionate to the incident, she knew; after all, she'd had no claim on him. Seeing him laughing with the lovely woman had brought its own brand of pain but had also ripped the scab off buried memories of Philippe's behaviour. *Never, never could she allow herself to fall for a man like that again.*

'Jesse hasn't mentioned any girls,' said Sandy slowly.

'Would he tell you?'

Sandy shook her head. 'I guess not. He seems to live by the code "a gentleman doesn't kiss and tell".'

'That's a good point in his favour. But there's no need for you to worry about me and Jesse. We've agreed we're going to try and be friends

as we're connected by family, but that's all.'
No-strings fun. That was how he'd described
it and it wouldn't happen again.

'Good,' said Sandy with rather too much
emphasis. 'Please keep it that way.'

'What do you mean?'

'Jesse is so not for you.'

Lizzie felt stung by Sandy's assumption. 'I
know that. I've figured it out all by myself. I
don't need my big sister to tell me,' she said
through gritted teeth. 'I am not interested in
Jesse as anything other than…than an acquaintance. Someone I have to try to be friends with
because you're married to his brother.' *She
would keep telling herself that.*

'I'm glad to hear it,' said Sandy with an air
of relief that Lizzie found more than a tad in-
sulting.

'By the way,' she said, 'thanks for not telling me Jesse would be here when I arrived in
Dolphin Bay.'

Sandy looked shamefaced. 'Yeah. That. I
didn't know he was going to injure his shoulder and land home here, did I? He's staying in
the converted boathouse where we lived before
we built the big house.'

'You could have warned me.'

'I was worried you'd get yourself wound up
at the thought of seeing him. I didn't want you

worrying about it. You've got enough on your plate.'

They'd always looked after each other and her sister's advice was well meant. 'Oh, Sandy, you don't have to worry about me. I've no intention of letting any guy get to me again.'

'After all you went through with Philippe, you know I can't help but worry about you. When I think of how you were in Sydney all by yourself having the baby while he—'

Lizzie put up her hand to stop her sister's flow of words. She didn't want to even think about that time, let alone talk about it. 'I'm older and wiser now. And much, much tougher.'

'Maybe I was wrong not to warn you about Jesse being home in Dolphin Bay.'

'No. You were right. It did give me a shock to see him here. Then to find out I'll be working with him every day…' *Maybe if she'd known, she'd have found a way to put off the opening of the café until Jesse had gone.*

'Don't knock back any offers of help—even if you don't particularly want to spend time with Jesse,' said Sandy. 'It's a big ask to get this café open for business in seven days. Besides, he's only here for a few weeks.'

'Four, to be precise,' Lizzie said. 'But don't worry, Sandy. I've got very good at resisting temptation. Jesse Morgan is no danger to my heart, I can assure you. I promise I'll make an effort to get along with him for your sake.'

CHAPTER FIVE

JESSE HADN'T LIVED in Dolphin Bay for any
length of time for years. If he took the new job
he'd been offered in Houston, Texas, he'd rarely
be back to his home town. Yet he took pride
in showing Lizzie more of the area where he,
his father and his grandfather had grown up.

He had seen so many parts of the world
devastated by floods, tornadoes, earthquakes
and other disasters he never took its beauty
for granted. No matter the growth of the town
itself, the heritage-listed harbour, the beaches
and the national park bushland stayed reassur-
ingly the same. Whatever the ups and downs
of his life, he took comfort from that.

'All I've seen of this part of the world is the
town, the beach and the road in and out,' Lizzie
said when she settled into the SUV he'd borrowed from his father. She was wearing white
jeans and a simple knit top that gave her a look
of cool elegance, of discreet sexiness he found

very appealing. 'I'm looking forward to seeing more.'

'Then we'll drive the long way around to the places we're going to visit,' he said.

Spring was his favourite time here, the quiet months before the place became overrun with summer tourists. The bush was lush with new growth, a haze of fresh green splashed with the yellow of spring-flowering wattle. The ocean dazzled in its hues of turquoise reflecting cloudless skies; the sand almost white under the sun.

After they'd left the town centre behind, he drove along the road that ran parallel to the sea and stopped at the rocky rise that gave the best view right down the length of Silver Gull, the beach south of Big Ray. He was gratified when Lizzie caught her breath at her first sight of the rollers crashing on the stretch of pristine sand, the stands of young eucalypt that grew down to the edge of it. He owned a block of land on the headland that looked right out to the ocean. One day he'd build a house there.

'I don't know if you've been away long enough to be impressed that in the evening kangaroos sometimes come down to splash in the shallows,' he said.

Her smile was completely without reticence. 'I would never not be impressed by that. If I saw kangaroos there now, I'd go crazy with my phone camera. My French friends would go crazy too when I sent them the photos.'

'You might want to bring your daughter down one evening,' he said, smiling at her enthusiasm, as he put the car into gear and pulled away.

'Amy would love that, and so would I,' she said. 'Our Aussie beaches were one of the things I really missed when I was living in France.'

'France must have had its advantages,' he said, tongue-in-cheek.

'Of course it did. Not just the food but also the fashion, the architecture—I loved it. Thought I would always live there.' He didn't miss the edge of sadness to her voice.

'I'm sorry it didn't work out,' he said.

'Thank you,' she murmured and turned her head to look out of the window, but not before he saw the bleakness in her eyes.

He'd like to know what had gone wrong with her marriage. What kind of a jerk would let go a woman like Lizzie and her cute little daughter? But it wasn't his business. And he didn't want to talk on an intimate level with her. Not when he was determined to deny any attraction he still felt for her.

'If I remember right you used to surf when

you were a teenager,' she said after a pause that was starting to feel uncomfortable.

'Correct,' he said. 'I was a crazy kid, always looking for bigger waves, greater challenges. My first year of university, a group of us went down to Tasmania to surf Australia's wildest waves. It was a wonder none of us was killed.'

'Would you do that now?'

'Go surfing?' he said, deliberately misunderstanding her question. 'Not without a wetsuit. The water's still too cold.'

'I meant surf those extreme waves. I couldn't imagine anything more terrifying.'

Should he share his worst ever surfing story with her? The experience that had completely changed his life? He wanted to keep the time he spent with her on an impersonal level. But now that she'd dropped her chilly persona, he found her dangerously easy to talk to. 'I lost my taste for extreme surfing when I had to outrun a tsunami.'

She laughed in disbelief. 'You were surfing a tsunami? C'mon, pull the other leg.'

'Not surfing. Running. Literally running away from the beach as a monster wave thundered in.'

'You're serious!'

'You bet I am.' Even now his gut clenched with terror and he gripped hard on the steering wheel at the memory of it. 'I took a gap year when I finished my engineering degree. Thought I'd surf my way around all the great breaks of the world. This particular beach was on the south coast of Sri Lanka. That morning I came out very early to surf. The boy who manned the amenities hut screamed at me to get off the beach and to run to the high ground with him.'

She gasped. 'That must have been terrifying.'

'His village was wiped out. But he saved my life. I stuck around to help in any way I could. The organisation I work for now came to rebuild and there was lots of work for a volunteer engineer. When we were done, they offered me a paying job.'

'That's quite a story,' she said. 'I wondered how you'd got into your line of work.' He felt her eyes on him but he kept his straight ahead on the road. 'The thing is, you don't look like a do-gooder type.'

Her comment so surprised him, he took his hands off the wheel for a second and had to quickly correct the swerve of the car. 'And what does a do-gooder look like?'

'Not like he could be an actor or a model. Not like...like you.'

He laughed. 'It doesn't matter what you look like when people need help.'

He knew he hadn't been hit with the ugly stick so didn't demur with false modesty when people commented on the fortunate combination of genes he'd been blessed with. Your looks you were born with. He'd learned it was the personality you developed that counted. Lizzie, for example, was turn-heads lovely but it was her energy and warmth that had drawn him to her. Camilla had been older than him, eye-catching rather than beautiful, but her smarts and confidence had drawn him to her.

'Is that why you do it? To help people? When a guy like you could do anything he wanted?'

'What else?' He went to shrug but winced at the resulting pain in his shoulder. 'That first project—the camaraderie, seeing people rehoused so quickly, it was a high. I wanted more.'

The tsunami had cured him of his adrenalin-junkie taste for extreme sports. The surfing on five-metre waves, the heli-skiing on avalanches, the mountain biking off the sides of mountains. After seeing real disaster he no longer wanted to court it in the name of sport.

But recently he'd been wondering if he had replaced one sort of thrill for another. The thrill of being called to dangerous sites of recent catastrophes, the still present danger, the high of being needed. It was a rewarding life. But he gave up a lot to do it. Regular hours, a permanent home. Of course that made for a convenient excuse to stay single. But Lizzie was the last person he wanted to discuss that with.

'It must be dangerous and uncomfortable at times,' she said. 'I admire you. I don't think I could do it. The world is lucky to have people like you.'

He liked that she got it. Seemed that Lizzie took people for what they were.

'When it all boils down to it, it's a job the same as any other,' he said. 'Not, perhaps, one I'd want to do for the rest of my life. But one I've been glad to do while I can.'

'I don't believe that for a moment. It's like a calling.'

'Maybe,' he said, not wanting to be drawn further into a conversation that might have him facing awkward truths about his motivations.

He distracted Lizzie by pointing to a flock of multi-coloured rainbow lorikeets hanging upside down off the branches of an indigenous grevillea bush. They were intoxicated by a surfeit of spring nectar from its spiky orange blossoms. When he and Ben had been kids, they'd found the sight of drunken parrots hilarious.

He was gratified when Lizzie found it funny too. And tried not to be entranced at the sight and sound of her laughter.

Lizzie carefully stacked her finds into the back of Jesse's SUV, feeling more excited about the café than she had since she'd arrived in Dolphin Bay. Jesse had driven her through unsealed roads that twisted through acres of bushland to a property where the parents of one of Jesse's old school friends had a beekeeping business.

On the spot she'd bought honey harvested from bees that had feasted on blossoms of the eucalypts growing in the adjoining national park and named for the trees: Spotted Gum, Iron Bark, River Gum.

Jesse seemed bemused she'd bought so many jars. 'This is liquid gold,' she explained as he slammed shut the door of the boot. 'Each honey has a particular flavour and they're not always available. I'm thrilled to bits. It's also considerably cheaper buying it direct from the farmer.'

'Your head is buzzing with ideas on what to cook with all this?' he asked.

She smiled at his joke and he met her smile with one of his own. When she'd first climbed into his car this morning she'd felt tense and on edge in his company but had gradually relaxed to the point she felt she could have a normal conversation without being choked by self-consciousness. 'You could say that. I love to cook with honey but I also like to drizzle it over, say, baked ricotta for breakfast.'

'Ricotta cheese for breakfast! A hungry man coming into the café won't think much of that.'

'How about served with a stack of buttermilk pancakes?'

'With a side of bacon?'

'With a side order of bacon,' she said.

'Much better,' he said. 'I like a big breakfast to start the day. I might become a regular customer while I'm in town.'

There was something very appealing about a big man with a hearty appetite. She remembered—

No! She would not even *think* about Jesse in relation to other appetites. Not for the first time she thanked heaven that her time with him at the wedding had been interrupted. She might have been very, very tempted to go much further than kisses and that would have been a big mistake of the irredeemable kind. Mere kisses were easy to put behind her. *Though not without a degree of regret that they could never take up where they'd left off.*

'Why not?' she said lightly. 'I guarantee

we'll have the best breakfasts and lunches in town. If you're still hungry after one of my breakfasts I'll give you your money back.'

'Is that a challenge?'

'An all-you-can-eat challenge? You'll just have to wait and see the food, won't you?'

'What about the coffee? A café will live or die on its coffee.'

'The beans they're ordering for me through the Harbourside are single origin beans from El Salvador and Guatemala. Fair trade, of course. I have no quibble with them.' Her voice trailed away at the end. She'd decided not to complain too much about anything to Jesse in case it found its way back to Ben and Sandy.

He turned to her. 'You don't sound as confident about the coffee as you do about the food.'

'How did you know that?'

'Just an edge to the tone of your voice.'

It was scary how quickly he'd learned to read her. Was that the Jesse way with women? Or a genuine friendship building between them? Still, she decided to confide in him— this was just business. 'You're right. We've got a state-of-the-art Italian coffee machine. But I'm not sure how good the girl is we've employed to use it.'

'If she's no good, employ someone else,' he

said, again displaying the ruthless business streak that surprised her.

'Easier said than done in a place like Dolphin Bay. There's not a lot of need for highly skilled baristas; as a result there aren't many to call upon.'

'I'm sure you'll sort it out,' he said. 'You're likely to have a few teething problems to overcome.'

'But I don't want teething problems,' she said stubbornly. 'I want the café to run perfectly from the get-go.'

'You really are a perfectionist, aren't you?'

'Yes,' she admitted. 'Which isn't always a good thing. It means I'm often disappointed.'

She knew there was a bitter edge to her words but she couldn't help it. *'No man is perfect,'* Philippe had shouted at her when she'd refused to take him back that final time. Was it so unreasonable to want a man who wouldn't cheat and lie? Who could manage to stay faithful?

Another reason to keep Jesse strictly hands-off. He was a player like Philippe. With all the potential for heartbreak that came with that kind of guy.

She forced herself away from old hurts and back to the café.

'Tell me if you think this is a good idea—

I want to ask your mother if she could share some of her favourite recipes from the old guest house. It would be nice to have that link to the Morgans in the café menu.'

Morgan's Guest House had been such a wonderful place, especially for a girl interested in cooking. Maura was an exceptional home-style cook.

Jesse paused for a long moment before he replied. She wondered if it had been a bad idea. She let out her breath when he answered, not realising she had been holding it. 'It's a great idea,' he said slowly. 'I'm sure Mum would be flattered. I'd certainly like it.'

'I'm so glad you think so,' she said with a rush of relief. 'I have such happy memories of helping Maura cook in the kitchen. She taught me to make perfect scrambled eggs. I've never found a better technique than hers.'

'When my mother heard you'd become a chef she was tickled pink that she might have had an influence on you.'

'I'm glad to hear that, because she was a big influence. My own mother encouraged me too.'

'And your father?'

She looked away from the car so she didn't have to face him. 'You've probably heard something from Sandy about what my father was like,' she said stiffly.

'Ben said Dr Randall Adam was an officious, domineering snob who—'

Lizzie put up her hand to halt him. 'Don't say it. After all he's done, he's still my father.'

'Sure,' he said, and she felt embarrassed at the sympathy in his voice. She didn't want him to feel sorry for her.

She scuffed at the ground near the back tyres of the car with the toe of her sneaker. 'Shall we say, he was less than encouraging when I didn't want to follow the academic path he'd mapped out for me. I wasn't the honours student Sandy was but he didn't get that. He wanted me to go to university. When I landed an apprenticeship at one of the most highly regarded restaurants in Sydney he didn't appreciate what a coup that was. He…well, he pretty much disowned me.'

Under threat of being kicked out of home without a cent to support her if she didn't complete her schooling, she'd finished high school. But the kitchen jobs she'd worked during her vacations had only reinforced her desire to become a chef. When she'd got the apprenticeship at the age of seventeen her father had carried out his threat and booted her out of home. It had backfired on him, though. Her mother had finally had enough of his bullying and infidelities. He went. Lizzie stayed. It was a triumph for her but one she hadn't relished—she'd adored her father and had been heartbroken.

Jesse shook his head in obvious disbelief. 'Isn't he proud of what you've achieved now?'

It was an effort to keep her voice steady. 'He sees being a chef as a trade rather than a profession. I...I think he's ashamed of me.' She shrugged. 'That's his problem, isn't it?'

'And not one you want to talk about, right?' Jesse said, his blue eyes shrewd in their assessment of her mood.

She had to fight an urge to throw herself into his arms and feel them around her in a big comforting hug. At Sandy's wedding ceremony she'd sobbed, not just with joy for her sister but for the loss of her own marriage and her own dreams of happiness. Jesse had silently held her and let her tears wet his linen shirt. She could never forget how it had felt to rest against his broad, powerful chest and feel his warmth and strength for just the few moments she had allowed herself the luxury. *It had meant nothing.*

'That's right,' she said. Then gave a big sigh.

'I won't say it doesn't still hurt. But I'm a big girl now with a child of my own to raise.'

'And you're sure as heck not going to raise her like you were raised,' he said.

'You're sure right on that,' she said with a shaky laugh.

'I was so lucky with my parents,' said Jesse. 'They're really good people who love Ben and me unconditionally. I didn't know what a gift that was until I grew up.'

'Looking back, I realise how kind Maura was,' Lizzie said. 'She must have found me a terrible nuisance, always underfoot. But there was so much tension between my parents, I wanted to avoid them. And Sandy was always off with Ben.'

'Of course she wouldn't have found you a nuisance,' said Jesse. 'Out of all the guests she had over the years, Mum always remembered you and Sandy. I think she'd love to share her recipes with you. Maybe…maybe it's time to revive some happy memories of the guest house.'

They both fell silent. Ben's first wife and baby son had died when the old guest house had burned down. That meant Jesse had lost his sister-in-law and nephew. She wondered how the tragedy had affected him. But it wasn't the kind of thing she felt she could ask. Not now. Maybe never.

'Can you ask about the recipes for me?' she said.

'Sure. Though I'm sure Mum would love it if you called her and asked her yourself.'

'I just might do that.'

Jesse glanced at his watch.

'I know, the two hours,' she said, resisting the urge to ask him just what catastrophe would befall him if he spent longer than that in her company. 'We'd better hurry up and get back in the car.' She walked around to the passenger side, settled into her seat and clicked in her seat belt. 'We're heading for a dairy next, right?'

'Correct,' said Jesse from the driver's seat. 'The farmer and his wife are old schoolfriends of mine. I hear they've won swags of awards for their cheeses and yogurts. I thought that might interest you.'

She turned to look at him, teasing. 'How do you know exactly what I need, Jesse Morgan?'

He held her gaze with a quizzical look of his own. 'Do I?' he said in that deep voice that sent a shiver of awareness down her spine.

Shocked at her reaction, she rapidly back-pedalled. 'In terms of supplies for the café, I meant.'

His dark brows drew together. 'Of course you did,' he said. 'What else would you have meant?'

She kept her gaze straight ahead and didn't answer.

CHAPTER SIX

THE SATURDAY TASTE-TESTING brunch at the café was in full swing. Bay Bites was packed with people, most of whom Lizzie didn't recognise, all of whom she wanted to impress. She'd spent all of Friday prepping food and working with the staff Sandy had hand-picked for her. They'd bonded well as a team, united by enthusiasm for the new venture. Now it was actually happening and it was exhilarating and scary at the same time.

She took a moment out from supervising her new kitchen staff to stand back behind the dolphin-carved countertop and watch what had turned into a party of sorts.

So far, so good. Her menu choices were getting rave reviews. She'd decided to serve small portions from the basic menu, handed around from trays, so people could try as many options as possible. She'd gone as far as printing feedback sheets to be filled in but the Dolphin

Bay taste-testers were proving more informal than that. They simply told her or the wait staff what they thought. She took their suggestions on board with a smile.

'I'd go easy on the chilli in that warm chicken salad, love,' Jesse's seventy-five-year-old great-aunt Ida said. 'Some of us oldies aren't keen on too much of the hot stuff.'

'The only problem with those little burgers was there weren't enough of them,' said the bank manager, a friend of Ben. 'Your other greedy guests emptied the tray.'

'The triple chocolate brownies? Bliss,' said one well-dressed thirty-plus woman. 'I'll be coming here for my book club meetings—it's ideal with the bookshop next door.'

Lizzie soon sensed an immense goodwill towards the new venture. Not, she realised, because of any reputation of hers. Because of Ben and Sandy, she was accepted as a member of the well-loved Morgan clan.

And then there was the Jesse effect. A number of these people were the wedding guests who had discovered her and Jesse kissing on the balcony. She was, and always would be in their eyes, one of 'Jesse's girls' and included in their general affection towards him. Who would have thought it?

From her corner behind the counter, she

watched Jesse as he worked the room, towering head and shoulders above most of the guests. Was he aware of how many female eyes followed him? Her eyes were among them. No matter where he was in the café she was conscious of him. It was as if he had some built-in magnet that drew female attention. She was no more immune than the rest of them. She just had to continue to fight it if she was going to be able to work with him.

He'd insisted on wearing the same blue jeans, white T-shirt and butcher-striped full apron in sea tones of blue and aqua as the wait staff. How could a guy look so hot in such pedestrian work-wear? But then a guy as handsome and well-built as Jesse would look good in anything. *Or nothing.* She shook her head to rid both her brain and her libido of such subversive thoughts. Jesse was off-limits—even to her imagination.

He'd arrived this morning before anyone else. 'I'm here to help,' he'd said. 'If I wear the uniform, people will know it.'

'I thought you were here to taste the food,' she'd protested as he'd tied on the apron, succeeding in looking utterly masculine as he did so. The colours of the stripes made his impossibly blue eyes look even bluer.

'I can do both,' he'd said in a tone that brooked no argument.

She'd let it go at that, in truth grateful for the extra help. And he had excelled himself. It appeared he knew most of the guests—and if he didn't he very soon did. Through the hum of conversation, the clatter of cutlery, the noise of chairs scraping on the tiled floor, she could hear the deep tones of his voice as he made people welcome to Bay Bites and talked up the food while he was at it.

If she had hired an expensive public relations consultant they wouldn't have done better than Jesse in promoting the new business.

She froze as she saw him bend his dark head to chat with Evie, the pretty blonde wife of the dairy farmer Jesse had introduced her to on Thursday. Straight away Lizzie had sensed that the girl was more than a mere acquaintance. Sure enough, it turned out she had dated Jesse in high school.

How many other women in this room had Jesse been involved with? *Was involved with right now?*

Was he really a player in the worst sense of the word, moving on once he'd made a conquest? Or was he just a natural-born charmer? She suspected the latter. The nurses in the hospital where he'd been born had probably gone gaga over him as he'd lain kicking and gurgling in his crib. And she'd bet he'd been a teacher's pet all the way through school—with the female teachers, anyway.

Evie had come to the taste-testing without her husband; rather she was accompanied by a curvy auburn-haired girl who was a friend visiting from Sydney. Lizzie gripped tight onto the edge of the counter as Evie's companion laughed up at Jesse. She schooled her face to show no reaction. He could talk and laugh with whatever woman he pleased. *It was nothing to her.*

That uncomfortable twinge of jealousy she felt as she watched them was further reason to keep Jesse at a distance.

Jealousy. She had battled hard with herself to overcome what she saw as a serious character flaw. As a child she'd been jealous of Sandy, not just for her toys or pretty dresses, but also because she'd been convinced her father loved Sandy more than he'd loved her. Thankfully, her mother had identified what was going on and made sure no rift ever developed between the sisters. She'd helped the young Lizzie learn to handle jealousy of other kids at school and later jealousy when she'd thought people at work had been favoured over her. As an adult,

Lizzie had thought the demon had been well and truly vanquished. Until she'd met Philippe.

She'd been just twenty-one and working at an upmarket resort in Port Douglas in tropical far northern Queensland. She had worked hard and played hard with talented young chefs from around the world on working holidays. Good-looking, charming Philippe had been way out of her league. But he'd made a play for her and she'd fallen hard for his French accent and his live-for-the-moment ways. It hadn't mattered that other girls never stopped flirting with him because he had assured her he loved only her. She'd followed him to France without a moment's hesitation.

But the jealousy demon had reared back into full flaming life after she'd given birth to Amy. For the first six months she'd been stuck at home living with his parents while he'd continued the work-hard-play-hard lifestyle they'd formerly enjoyed together. And Philippe had not been the type of man to do without feminine attention.

Just like Jesse, she thought now as he smiled at the auburn-haired girl who was hanging onto his every word. Who could blame the girl for being dazzled by his movie-star looks and genuine charm? *She couldn't let it get to her.* Women of all ages gravitated to Jesse and he gravitated to them. That was the way he was and it wasn't likely to change. It was the reason above all others that she could never be more than passing friendly with him.

If Jesse had been more than a friend, she would by now be racked with jealousy. It wasn't a feeling she enjoyed. She had hated the jealous, suspicious person she had become towards the end of her marriage; she never wanted to go there again.

Jesse must have felt her gaze on him because he said something to the two women, turned and headed towards her. He indicated his near-empty tray where a lone piece of chicken sat in a pile of baby spinach leaves. 'Want some?'

She shook her head. 'Can't eat. Too concerned with feeding all of this lot.'

'You're sure? You need to keep your energy up. It's delicious. Made with free-range chicken breast stuffed with organic caramelised tomato and locally produced goat's cheese and wrapped in Italian prosciutto.'

She smiled. 'You're doing a good job of selling it to me, but no thanks all the same.'

'Can't let it go to waste,' he said, popping it into his mouth.

'Glad you approve,' she said as he ate the chicken with evident relish. A similar dish had been one of the most popular items in the Sydney restaurant she'd worked in when she'd first come back from France. Served with a salad for lunch, she hoped it would be popular here too.

'The slow-cooked lamb was a huge success,' he said. 'Although some people said they'd prefer an onion relish to the beetroot relish.'

'*Some* people,' she said, arching her brow. 'How many people? One person in particular, perhaps?'

'One in particular has never much liked beetroot. He'd like the onion.'

'So maybe the chef was correct in her guess that that particular person would like the slow-cooked lamb?'

'Maybe.'

'You refuse to admit I was right about what you'd like best?'

'I haven't finished tasting everything yet. I'll let you know at the end. By the way, the asparagus and feta frittata was a big hit with the ladies. I told them it was low calorie, though I don't know whether that's actually true.'

Was he born with an innate knowledge of what appealed to women? Or was it some masculine dark art he practised to enchant and ensnare them? *She could not let herself fall under his spell—it would be only too easy.*

'Make sure you don't miss out on the apple

pie, I'm sure you'll love it,' she said. 'But don't even think of telling anyone it's low calorie. I might get sued when my customers start stacking on the weight.'

He put down the tray, leaned across the counter towards her and spoke in a low voice, his eyes warm with what seemed like genuine concern. 'Seriously, are you pleased how it's going?'

She nodded. 'Really pleased. I don't want to jinx myself but people are booking already for our opening day on Thursday.'

'The buzz is good. I was on door duty a while ago and had to turn passers-by away. Lucky we put the "Closed for Private Function" sign on the door or I reckon we'd have been invaded.'

· 'I've handed out a lot of leaflets letting people know about the opening hours and menu.'

'So everything is going as planned?'

'I'm happy but—'

'You're not happy with the staff.'

Again, she was surprised at how easily he read her. Especially when he scarcely knew her. 'No. Yes. I mean I'm really happy with the sous chef. He's excellent. In fact he's too good for a café and I doubt we'll keep him.' She glanced back at the kitchen. But with the noise level of the café there was no way the chef could hear her.

'You'll keep him. He's already got one kid and another on the way. He can't afford to leave Dolphin Bay.'

'I don't know whether to be glad for us or sad for him.'

'Try glad for him. He's happy to have a job in his home town. What about the others?'

'The kitchen hand is great with both prep and clearing up and the waitresses are enthusiastic and friendly, which is just what I want.'

'I can hear a "but" coming.'

'The waitress who is also the barista— Nikki. She's a nice girl but not nearly as experienced with making coffee as she said and I'm worried how she'll work under pressure.'

'You know what I said. With a small staff and a reputation to establish you can't afford any weak links.'

'I know. And...thanks for the advice.'

He picked up the tray again, swivelling it on one hand. 'The kitchen is calling.'

She'd noticed how adeptly he'd carried the tray, served the food. 'You know, if you weren't an engineer and helping the world, you'd have a great future in hospitality,' she teased.

'Been there. Done that. I worked as a waiter for an agency while I was at university. I'm only doing it again to help make Bay Bites a success.'

She bet she knew which agency. It employed only the handsomest of handsome men. It figured they'd want Jesse on their books even if only in university vacations.

Jesse took off again, stopping for a quick word with his mother on his way to the kitchen.

Lizzie waved to Maura, and Maura smiled and blew her a kiss. Jesse's mother was a tall, imposing woman with Jesse's blue eyes and black hair, though hers was now threaded with grey. Lizzie had taken up with her again as if it had been yesterday that she'd been a teenager helping her in the kitchen and soaking up the older woman's cooking lore.

Thankfully, Maura had been delighted at the idea of sharing some of the guest house favourites based on the cooking of her Irish youth. They'd made a date for Monday to go through the recipes. *Just to go through the recipes, not to talk about Jesse*, Lizzie reminded herself. Or to do anything as ridiculous as to ask Maura to show her his baby photos. Her thoughts of him being doted over as a baby had sparked a totally unwarranted curiosity to see what he'd looked like as a little boy.

As Jesse picked up a tray of mini muffins, he wondered what the heck he was doing playing at being a waiter in a café. He hadn't enjoyed the time he'd spent in the service industry during university, had only done it to fund his surfing and skiing trips. Being polite to ill-mannered clients of catering companies hadn't been at all to his liking. In fact he'd lost his job when he'd tipped a pitcher of cold water over an obnoxious drunken guest who wouldn't stop harassing one of the young waitresses. The agency had never hired him again and he hadn't given a damn.

He'd promised to help Sandy with the café but the building work he'd already done was more than his sister-in-law would ever have expected. No. He had to be honest with himself. This café gig was all about Lizzie. Seeing her every day. Being part of her life. And that was a bad, bad idea. Even for two hours a day.

Because he couldn't stop thinking about her. How beautiful she was. Her grace and elegance. Her warmth and humour. Remembering how she'd felt in his arms and how he'd like to have her there again. Her passionate response to his kisses and how he'd like—

In short, he was failing dismally in thinking of Lizzie Dumont as a family acquaintance trying to be friends. *Could it ever really be platonic between them?* There would always be an undercurrent of sexual attraction, of possibilities. Even in that white chef's jacket and baggy black pants she looked beautiful. He even found it alluring the way she tasted food in the kitchen—how she closed her eyes, the way she used her tongue, her murmurs of pleasure when the food tasted the way it should.

Lizzie wasn't sexy in a hip-swinging, cleavage-baring way. But there was something about the way she carried herself, the way she smiled that hinted at the passionate woman he knew existed under her contained exterior.

However, his reasons for not wanting to date her were still there and stopped him from flirting with her, from suggesting they see each other while he was in town. There could be no 'fun while it lasts' scenarios with Lizzie. And the alternative—something more serious—was not on for him. The last time he'd tried serious it had taken him years to recover from the emotional battering.

He had fallen so hard and fast for Camilla he hadn't seen sense. Hadn't realised when he'd talked to her about his feelings she had answered him with weasel words that had had him completely stymied, fooled into thinking she cared for him. He cringed when he thought about how naïve and idealistic he'd been. When he'd proposed to her she had virtually laughed in his face.

No way would he risk going there again with Lizzie. He had to stop looking at her, noticing her, admiring her.

There was also the sobering truth that Lizzie didn't seem to want anything to do with him other than as a family friend. In fact he suspected she disapproved of him.

He'd noticed the way she'd watched him as he'd worked the room, offering samples of food, talking up the café, Lizzie's skills as a chef, the bookshop next door, how it would all work when Bay Bites opened. He'd talked to guys too, but it was the women who'd wanted to linger and chat. As it always had been. And Lizzie was clocking that female attention.

Ever since he'd turned fourteen women had made it obvious they found him attractive. *'You don't even have to try, you lucky dog,'* Ben had often said when they were younger.

When his mates had been trying to talk girls into their beds he'd been trying to get them out of his. Literally. More than once he'd come home and found a girl he scarcely knew had climbed through his bedroom window and was waiting for him, naked in his bed.

He'd found that a turn-off rather than a turn-on. He'd had to ask them to leave in the nicest possible way without hurting their feelings.

When Jesse made love to a woman it was always going to be memorable—and his choice.

His brother Ben stopped him to snag first one muffin then another from his tray. 'Sure I can't convince you to stay in Dolphin Bay and work here? With your way with the ladies, I reckon we'll double the numbers of female customers. Look at them, flocking to your side like they've always done.'

'Ha ha,' he said, ignoring the bait, conscious that Lizzie might overhear the conversation with his brother.

As he'd said to Lizzie, his prowess with the opposite sex was greatly exaggerated. And he hadn't taken advantage of his gift with women. He had always been honest about his feelings. Dated one girl at a time. Made it clear when he wasn't looking for anything serious. Bailed before anyone got hurt. Let her tell everyone *she* had dumped *him*. Had stayed friends with his ex-girlfriends—as far as their boyfriends or husbands would allow.

But today, seeing himself through Lizzie's eyes, he wasn't so sure he was comfortable with all that any more. Most of his Dolphin Bay friends were married now. Though the guys moaned and complained about being tied down, he didn't actually believe them when they said they envied him his life. They seemed too content.

Now he sometimes wondered what they really thought about him being single as he faced turning thirty. He knew the townsfolk had laid bets on him always staying a bachelor. It was beginning to bug him. But he had never treated their interest in his ladies' man reputation as anything other than a laugh; never talked about the reasons he'd stayed on his own.

He hadn't told anyone in Dolphin Bay— even his family—about what had happened with Camilla. Had never confided how the deaths of his sister-in-law Jodi and little nephew Liam had affected him. How terrified he'd been at seeing Ben suffer the life-destroying pain caused by the loss of love. On the cusp of manhood, Jesse had resolved he would never endure what Ben had endured. He'd put the brakes on any relationship that threatened to get serious.

Gradually, however, he'd realised Ben's pain should not be his pain. That he had to love his own way, take his own risks. He'd let down his guard by the time he'd met Camilla and hurtled into a relationship with her. Only for her callous rejection of his love to send him right back behind his barricades.

Was that enough now?

He looked over to Lizzie but she had disappeared into the kitchen again. He'd seen yet another side of her today. Calm. Competent. Ruthlessly efficient under pressure. He liked it.

He admired her for her commitment. Surely a café serving toasted ham and cheese sandwiches—even if she called them *croque monsieur*—was a huge comedown for someone with Lizzie's career credentials. Dolphin Bay must be just a pit stop for Lizzie. She had a half-French daughter. How long before she got fed up with flipping fried eggs and turned her sights back to Europe?

Or did he have that wrong? It was logical for him to base future plans purely on his career. Maybe it wasn't so for Lizzie. She was a mother—perhaps that was why she could settle for Bay Bites? Maybe because it was in the best interests of her daughter.

He couldn't imagine how it would be to put someone else first. Wife. Child. Suiting himself had seemed just fine up to now. *A charming Peter Pan.* That was what Camilla had called him at their most recent encounter. She'd said it with a laugh. Hadn't meant it to sound like an insult. But it had stung just the same. And made him think.

He headed back into the fray. 'Be quick before these muffins are all snatched off the tray,' he said to the nice redhead friend of Evie's. 'They're made with organically grown rhubarb, locally produced sour cream—in fact from Evie's farm—and—'

The girl picked one up from the tray, sniffed it, broke off a piece, tasted it. 'And pure maple syrup from the forests of Quebec, if I'm not wrong—together with Queensland pecans,' she pronounced.

He stared at her, taken aback. 'Sounds good to me. I'll check with the chef.' He must ask Lizzie. He really wasn't cut out to be a waiter.

Lizzie slumped in one of the bentwood chairs, exhausted. The guests had gone. The clearing up was done. The staff dismissed. Only Sandy, Ben and Jesse remained.

Sandy was incandescent with joy. 'Ever since I first set foot in the bookshop, I dreamed of there being a café next door. If today was an indication of how it's going to turn out, I think my dream is on its way to coming true. Thanks to my sister.'

She grabbed both Lizzie's hands and pulled her to her feet. 'Hug,' she commanded. Lizzie smiled and did as she was told. If she could repay Sandy's kindness with a successful café she'd be happy.

'C'mon, Ben too,' said Sandy. 'And you, too, Jesse. Group hug. Family hug.'

Alarmed, Lizzie stiffened. 'I don't think—'

But, before she knew it, both she and Sandy were enveloped in a bear hug from tall, blond Ben whom she already loved as a brother. Then Jesse joined in and it was a different feeling altogether. Every nerve went on alert as she felt Jesse's strong arms around her, was pulled against the solid wall of his chest, breathed in his maleness and warmth. Could he feel her heart pounding at his nearness?

She could never, ever think of Jesse as a brother.

And right at this moment it was darn near impossible to think of him only as a friend.

CHAPTER SEVEN

THE NEXT DAY, mid-morning, Jesse drove from the boathouse where he was staying towards Silver Gull beach. He knew the surf would be flat with just the occasional swell; he'd checked it while he was on his early morning run just after dawn. But that didn't bother him. Surfing wasn't possible right now, with his shoulder injury. He couldn't paddle out to where the waves would usually be breaking and he couldn't use his shoulders to get him into a wave. That right shoulder was aching today. Carrying all those food-laden trays yesterday probably hadn't been the wisest thing he could have done in terms of shoulder rehabilitation.

But he could swim. Cautiously. No freestyle. But some breaststroke. Maybe some back-kick that left his shoulders right out of it. Heck, just to float around would be better than nothing.

The beach should be near-deserted at this time of morning. It wasn't as popular as Big

Ray, which was one of the reasons he liked it. All the early morning runners and dog walkers would have gone home by now and October wasn't yet peak swimming season. Although it was gloriously sunny, with very little breeze, the water was still too cold for all but the intrepid to swim without a wetsuit.

The first thing he saw as he approached the beach access was Lizzie's small blue hatchback parked carefully off the road. He didn't know whether to be glad or annoyed she was here. The more he saw of her, the more he was perturbed by his attraction to her. That group hug the night before had tested his endurance. Having Lizzie back in his arms—well, half of Lizzie considering the nature of a group hug—had brought desire for her rushing back in a major way. He hadn't stopped thinking about her since.

For a long moment he left the engine idling. Go or stay?

No contest, he thought as he killed the engine. It wasn't a good idea for Lizzie to be swimming by herself. Not at Silver Gull with its dangerous rip undertow that could pull an unwary swimmer out to sea. He needed to keep an eye on her, keep her safe. He zipped himself into his wetsuit, grabbed a towel and headed towards the sand dunes that bordered the southern end of the beach.

As he'd thought, there wasn't another soul there. Almost straight away he saw Lizzie on the sand halfway between where the gum trees grew down to the edge of the beach and where the small breaking waves swirled up onto the sand in lacy white foam. She was lying on her back on a bright pink towel, her lovely body covered only by a turquoise and white checked bikini. Her long slender limbs were stretched out in total relaxation, her pale hair loose and glinting like silver in the sunlight, an expression of bliss on her face.

Jesse clenched his fists by his sides and a cold sweat broke out on his forehead. It would have been better if he'd kept on driving and gone to a different beach.

He could not deny there had been times since he'd met Lizzie that he had wondered how she looked under her clothes. But the reality of her in the skimpy bikini far surpassed any fantasy—her breasts high and round, her hips flaring gently, her body slender not skinny. She was perfect in every way. He couldn't help but observe that she had certainly filled out since her teenage years.

He coughed to alert her to his presence, not wanting to be seen to stare at her for so long it could be perceived as untoward. Startled, she sat up quickly, looked up at him. She took off her sunglasses and then used her hand to shade her eyes, blinking to focus on him. 'Jesse. You…you surprised me.'

He wasn't sure whether it was shock or pleasure he saw in her eyes. 'Catching some rays?' he asked, trying to sound casual when all he could think about was how sexy she looked in that bikini. Of how, in fact, the design of a bikini didn't so much cover up but draw attention.

'I desperately need to get some colour,' she said, stretching out her arms with unconscious grace. 'Feeling the sun on my skin is heaven. There won't be much beach time once the café opens.'

Already the smooth skin of her shoulders was tinged with gold. 'Are you planning to swim?' he asked.

She turned to look towards the water, calm, translucent, sparkling in the sunlight as far as the eye could see. 'Just thinking about it now. The water looks so inviting.'

'It will be very cold in.'

She indicated the beach bag to the left side of the towel. 'I borrowed Sandy's wetsuit.'

He gritted his teeth. 'Might be an idea to put it on.'

'I will soon. I'm enjoying—'

'Put it on now, will you.' His voice came out harsher than he had intended.

She frowned. 'But—'

'I can't talk to you while you're wearing that bikini.' He spoke somewhere over her head, not trusting himself to look at her.

'But it's a modest bikini—'

'It does nothing to hide what a beautiful body you have. That's more than a guy who's trying to be just friends can take.'

'Oh,' she said and blushed so the colour on her cheeks rivalled that of her towel.

He tossed her his navy striped towel. 'Here. Cover up, will you.'

She caught the towel. 'Sure. I didn't think…' She pulled his towel around her, twisting to tuck it into her bikini top between her breasts. *Lucky towel.* Then she went to get up from the sand.

Automatically, he offered her his hand to help her. For a long moment she just stared at it with an expression he couldn't read. Then she put her narrow hand in his much larger one. He pulled her to her feet, unable to keep his eyes from how lovely she was.

She faced him, standing very still. She was tall, but he was taller and she had to look up to him, exposing her slender neck, her delicate throat where he could see a pulse throbbing. Their gazes locked. Her grey eyes seemed brighter, perhaps reflecting the blue of the sky and the sea. 'Thank you,' she murmured.

Jesse still held her hand and when she made no effort to free it he tightened his grip—now he had her so close he couldn't bear to let her go. He noticed a few grains of sand sprinkled on her cheek, maybe from where she'd pushed her hair away from her face. Reluctant to let go of her hand, he used his other hand to gently wipe off the tiny grains from where they adhered to her smooth skin.

She closed her eyes with a flutter of long fair lashes and he could feel her tremble beneath his touch as his fingers then traced down her cheek towards her mouth. He traced the outline of her soft, lovely mouth with his fingers and now it was he who trembled with awareness and a stunned disbelief she wasn't pushing him away.

Her lips parted just enough for her to breathe out a slow sigh and open her eyes. Jesse saw in them both wariness and desire. 'Jesse, I...' Whatever she might have been about to say faltered to nothing. She swayed towards him.

He dropped his hand and used it to take her other hand and pull her closer to him, so close he could feel the heat from her sun-warmed body. He pressed his mouth to hers in a soft questioning kiss—she gave him the answer he wanted with the pressure of her lips back on his. As he deepened the kiss he felt the same fierce surge of possessive hunger he'd felt the first time he'd kissed her. Had kissed her, then been parted from her through a stupid misunderstanding before he'd had the chance to think about what that flare of attraction between them could mean.

Six months between kisses and she tasted the same. Felt the same. And he wanted her just as much—more. She kissed him back with a fierce intensity that sent a surge of excitement pulsing through him. He dropped his hands so he could lock his arms around her. With a little murmur she wound her arms around his neck and pulled him close. The towel slid to the sand between them. 'Leave it,' he growled against her mouth then slanted and deepened the angle of his kiss.

The longing for her he'd been holding back overwhelmed him. All this platonic friendship stuff was bulldust as far as he was concerned. He'd wanted her from the time she'd first swept him up with her warmth and laughter, set him the challenge of that cool exterior and the promise of passion beneath. He slid his hands up her slender waist, skimmed her

small, firm breasts as her heart thudded under
his hand and she gasped under his mouth.

There were master chefs, master sommeliers,
master chocolatiers—but Jesse was truly a
master kisser, Lizzie mused, her thoughts
barely coherent through a fizz of excitement.
Delicious shivers of pleasure tingled across her
skin as Jesse worked seductive magic with his
lips and tongue. The scrape of the stubble on
his chin was an exciting contrast to the soft-
ness of his mouth; the hard strength of his body
to the tenderness of his hands on her bare skin.
The last man to kiss her had been Jesse six
months ago. The way he kissed her now was
everything she'd remembered, everything that
had excited her that night on the balcony and
awoken needs she'd tried to deny.

She'd been daydreaming about him when
she'd been lying on the beach—and then suddenly he'd been there, as if conjured up from
her fantasies. She was so dazed that before she
knew it she was in his arms, with no time to
worry about whether it was right, wrong or ill-
advised. Another public kiss with Jesse? Her
craving to be close to him was so strong the
possibility of being caught again, being teased
again, had scarcely registered.

Jesse looked so hot in that wetsuit, the tight

black fabric moulding his broad chest, flat belly, muscular limbs. Unshaven, his black hair carelessly tousled as if he'd just run his hand through it in his hurry to get to the beach, he'd never looked more should-be-on-billboards handsome. When he'd taken her hand to help her up from the sand, she'd known where it would lead. Known and felt dizzy with anticipation.

Now she kissed him back, lost in the overwhelming pleasure of being with Jesse again. She'd found it impossible to clamp down on her attraction to him—no matter how many times she'd told herself Jesse wasn't right for her. She might be able to deny herself that Belgian chocolate—but not this.

Desire bloomed in the tightening of her nipples, the ache to be closer, and she tightened her arms around his neck, breathing in the intoxicating scent of his skin. Wanting him. Craving more than kisses. She had never been kissed the way Jesse kissed. Jesse the master kisser would be Jesse the master lover and she shivered in sensual anticipation of the discovery.

What was she thinking? She stilled in his embrace.

She could not let herself want Jesse this much. Too many other women wanted Jesse.

It would only lead to heartbreak, to agony. *He couldn't give her what she needed.*

She broke the kiss and drew away, pushing against his chest, her breath ragged. He murmured a protest and gathered her back into his arms but he let her go when she continued to maintain her resistance. His expression, passion fading to bewilderment and—yes—hurt wrenched at her heart. She hated that she was the cause of that.

What had just happened was purely physical, she reminded herself. Oh, she wanted Jesse all right. And the more she'd got to like him, the more she'd wanted him. But she needed to be cherished, loved for herself, not be the latest in a line of conquests. She wanted to love and be loved—but she also wanted to trust.

How hard would it be to trust a player again?

'Jesse, I can't do this. I won't do this.' Her voice came out wobblier than she would have liked. But Jesse got the message.

He choked out just the one word. 'Why?'

Jesse gulped in deep breaths of salt-tangy air to try and get back his equilibrium. He was convinced that Lizzie had enjoyed being with him as much as he'd enjoyed being with her. He could see her aroused nipples through the fabric of her bikini top. She was flushed, her eyes dilated, her mouth swollen from his kisses. She had never looked lovelier.

But she turned away from him. Bent down and picked up his towel where it lay rumpled on the sand at her feet. With hands that weren't steady she draped it around her shoulders but it covered less than it revealed. *He wanted her so much it hurt.*

She twisted the corner of the towel until it was scrunched into a knot, untwisted it and twisted it again before she looked back up at him. 'Because all those reasons that make it a bad idea for us to get together are still there,' she said.

Somewhere in the realm of good sense he knew that. Hell, he had his reasons too. Desire this strong could lead to pain as wrenching as Camilla had inflicted on him. But his body didn't want to listen to his brain. He wanted Lizzie and he wanted her now. If not now this afternoon, this evening, tonight—and hang the consequences.

'It was…a mistake. We have to forget it happened. This…this shouldn't ch-change anything between us,' she stammered.

He cleared his throat. 'How can it *not* change things between us?'

She looked up at him, her eyes huge in the oval of her face. 'Jesse, I want you so much I'm aching for you.' Her voice caught and she took in a deep breath but it did nothing to steady it. 'If…if things were different there's nothing more I'd want than to make love with you right now.'

He made a disbelieving grunt in response.

'Oh, not on the beach. But back in my apartment. In a hotel room. At your place. Somewhere private where we could explore each other, please each other, satisfy our curiosity about each other. Even…even if that was all we ever had.'

He groaned and when he spoke his voice was edged with anger. 'Do you realise what you're doing talking to me like that? Don't be a—'

'A tease? Believe me, I'm not teasing.' She swallowed hard. 'In the six months since I last saw you, even though I thought you'd gone off with another woman, I dreamed of you. I kept waking up from dreams of you. Wanting you. Aching for you. Reaching for you, to find only an empty bed.'

'Then why—?'

'Because desire isn't enough.' She took in another of those deep breaths that made her breasts swell over her bikini top in such a tantalising way. 'I'm sometimes accused of being blunt but I have to be honest with you,' she said.

He swallowed a curse word. Whenever anyone used that 'honest' phrase he knew he was about to hear something he didn't want to hear. Lizzie's expression didn't give him cause to think otherwise.

'Fire away,' he said through gritted teeth.

'I've told you, right now there's no room in my life for a man.' She was having trouble meeting his eyes. Not a good sign. 'But if I do start to date again, I want it to be someone… someone serious, dependable, reliable. Not—'

'Not someone like me,' he finished for her, his voice brusque.

She bit her lip. 'That didn't come out well, did it?' she said with a quiver to her voice. 'It's not that you're not gorgeous. You are. In fact you're too gorgeous.'

'I don't know how being told I'm gorgeous sounds like an insult, but I get the gist of it.'

Her eyes widened. 'I didn't want that to sound like an insult. I wouldn't want to hurt you for the world.'

I wouldn't want to hurt you for the world. Jesse felt uncomfortably aware that he had used something like that phrase more than once when kindly breaking up with a woman. But those words directed at him did not feel good. They made him feel scorned like he'd felt when Camilla had rejected him—though she hadn't been as kind about it as Lizzie was being.

'No offence taken,' he said gruffly.

'I…I'm not very good at this,' she said, looking down at the ground, scuffing the sand with her bare foot.

Amazing that while she was thrusting the knife deep into his gut and then twisting it, he felt sorry for her having to deliver the message. In the interests of being *honest*.

'No one is good at it,' he said.

'I do want to try to explain. Because…because I've come to really like you.'

Like. It was a runner-up word. A consolation prize word. A loser word. How could he have exposed himself again to this?

'Continue,' he said gruffly.

'My ex was a good-looking guy with the charisma to go with it. I was always having to look over my shoulder to see what woman was pursuing him, what woman he was encouraging.'

'He was a *player*, right?' He practically spat out that word he was getting sick of hearing applied to him.

She nodded. 'I never want to endure a relationship with someone like that again. I can't live with that feeling that I'm not the only woman in my man's life. To be always suspicious of girls he works with, girls he encounters anywhere. I want to come first, last and in between with a man. Not…not always feeling humiliated and rejected.'

Jesse clenched his fists by his sides. He wasn't that guy. How could she be so wrong about him? A nagging inner voice gave him the answer. *Because that's the way you appear.* He'd done such a good job of acting the player to cover up his fears and pain that he'd given Lizzie the wrong impression of him.

It was true, over the years he'd been flattered by all that female attention. *But he didn't want it now.* He didn't want people taking bets on his marital status. Most of all he didn't want Lizzie so unfairly lumping him in a category of cheats and heartbreakers.

'What makes you think I'm like your ex-husband? You're implying that he cheated on you—I've never cheated or been unfaithful to a girlfriend. *Never.*'

'I…I believe you,' she said but her eyes told a different story. She'd stuck him in the same category as her ex and nothing he'd done—or the reputation he had acquired—had changed her mind.

He was not the guy she thought he was. He had to prove that to her.

'What happened at the wedding to cause you to think I'd gone off with another woman was a misunderstanding,' he said. 'So what makes you think I live up to my reputation?'

Her smile was shaky. 'Women adore you. Not just young attractive women who want to date you. Older women dote on you. Ex-girlfriends like Evie want you still in their life. Even children are fans. Amy was beside herself with excitement when I told her on the phone last night that Uncle Jesse would be here when she got back from France. You were such a hit with her at the wedding when you danced her right around the room.'

He frowned. 'And that's a bad thing? Would you prefer I was the kind of guy women loathed? Feared even?'

'Of course not.' She shook her head as if to clear her thoughts. 'I'm not getting this across at all well, am I? Fact is, it's not all about you; it's—'

He put up his hand. 'Whoa. If you're going to say "it's not you; it's me" forget it, I don't want to hear that old cliché.'

'What I'm trying to tell you is that I…I'm a jealous person.' She looked down at her feet for a moment as if she was ashamed of her words before she faced him again. 'A jealous woman and a chick-magnet guy are not a good combination, as I found out in my marriage. It wasn't just his infidelity that ended it; my jealousy and suspicion made it impossible for us to live with each other.'

'In my book, infidelity is unforgivable.' He clenched his jaw.

She looked across him and out to sea as if gathering her words before she faced him again. 'There…there can be shades of grey…'

He shook his head. 'Fidelity is non-negotiable. No cheating, end of story. If either party cheats—the relationship is over. For good.'

Did she believe him? Or had she heard too many lies from that ex-husband to believe an honest guy?

Her brow furrowed. 'That stance is not…not what I would have expected of you.'

'You've been listening to gossips.' He snorted in disgust. 'What would they know about my private life? You think I don't know about betrayal? You think I haven't been hurt?'

'I…I only know what I've heard.' She bit down on her lower lip, her face a picture of misery.

'I thought I'd found the woman I wanted to be with for the rest of my life. Turned out she was a cheat and a liar. But I don't lie or cheat. Never have. Never will.'

'I'm sorry, Jesse, if I got it wrong. But I can't take risks when it comes to men. For my sake and for my daughter's.' Only then came that familiar tilt to her chin. 'No matter how much I might want that man.'

He glanced down at the small scars on her hands and forearms. Scars she'd got in the kitchen, she'd told him, from burning oil and scalding steam and knives that had slipped. Now he realised she had scars on the inside too. Her ex-husband—and maybe before that her father—had chipped away at her trust, at her belief that she could inspire lasting love and fidelity. *That she deserved to be cherished and honoured.*

Whoa. He wasn't thinking the L word here. Just the crazy attraction. Then the friendship. And the other L word. He realised how much in these last few days he had grown to like and admire Lizzie. In this context, 'like' was not a loser word. It was a feeling that built on that instant physical attraction to something that packed a powerful punch.

Lizzie was right—the reasons they both had for keeping the other at friend status were still there. He didn't want to put his heart on the line again and he didn't want to risk wounding her with further scars.

He ached to take her in his arms again but had no intention of doing so. It wasn't what she wanted. She didn't need a man like him in her life.

'I'd like to give you a big hug but…but I don't think it's a good idea,' he said, trying to sound offhand but failing dismally, betrayed by the hitch in his voice.

Warm colour flushed her cheeks. 'I agree. And…and no more kissing. I can't deal with how it makes me feel.'

He realised how vulnerable she was under that blunt-speaking front.

'No more kissing,' he agreed though he hated the idea of never being able to kiss her again.

She looked up at him, eyes huge, hair a silver cloud around her face. 'Jesse, I…I wasn't lying when I said how much I liked you. I do count you as a friend now.'

He nodded. 'Yeah. I like you too. We're friends.' But he didn't offer his hand to shake on it. No touching. No kissing. No physical contact of any kind. That was how it would have to be. No matter how difficult that stance would be to maintain when he had to see her every day.

He looked towards the water. It was still a low swell. Still good for swimming. And he needed to get in there. Physical activity was always his way of dealing with stress and difficult situations. 'Are you going to swim?' he asked her.

She shook her head. 'I should be getting back to the café.'

Good. He didn't want her to join him in that water. Splashing around with her in a wetsuit moulded close to her curves would be more than he could endure.

'I'm going in,' he said. 'This is my favourite beach and I want to spend as much time as I can here while I'm home.'

She walked back to where her towel and bag were on the sand. She picked up her pink towel and turned her back to him as she swapped his towel for hers. Her back view was beautiful, with her hair tumbling around her shoulders, her narrow waist and shapely behind. *He wanted her but he couldn't have her.* He turned his head away. 'Just leave my towel there,' he said gruffly.

'Will you…will you be coming to the café today?' she asked, facing him again.

He hadn't given her two hours of help today but he needed distance from her. 'No. I'm driving to Sydney tonight.'

'Oh,' she said.

'I've got an appointment tomorrow with the orthopaedic specialist for my shoulder,' he said. And he had a video interview with the executives of the company in Houston. 'I'll see you when I get back.'

He was going to find it difficult working those two hours a day with her for the rest of his time back home in Dolphin Bay. But he had a commitment to Sandy that he would honour. He also wanted to be a friend to Lizzie now that they'd got this far.

But if she was to respect him as something other than a good-looking player—even in the context of a family connection friendship—he had to prove that the Jesse of his reputation and the real Jesse were not one and the same.

CHAPTER EIGHT

It WAS SEVEN o'clock on the morning of the official opening of Bay Bites and the café doors were due to open in half an hour for their very first breakfast service. Lizzie had been working in the kitchen since five. She was confident she and her team had done all they could to prepare but still she was so nervous she had to keep wiping her hands down the side of her apron.

She'd worked at a start-up before. But not as the person in charge. It was a very different matter taking orders in the kitchen from someone else compared to being the one responsible for the success or failure of the venture. She twirled that piece of her hair that always escaped when she tied back her hair so hard it tugged at her scalp and made her wince. *What if no one showed up?*

That line of thought was crazy; she knew that—they had confirmed bookings for breakfast, brunch and lunch. Okay, so some of them were Morgan family and friends who had promised to be there to show support. But they would only be there the first few days; after that it would be up to word-of-mouth and reputation for the business to work.

Sandy, whose background was in advertising and marketing, had told her not to worry about all that—it was up to her to promote the new business. It was up to Lizzie to make the food—and the coffee—good enough for people to return again and again. It was all about the food, Sandy had said several times.

Lizzie took a deep steadying breath. She was confident the food was good, that she could hold up her end of the deal. Service had to be good too. Fingers crossed that Nikki, the young barista, could deal with the pressure.

She kept looking up to see if any early customers had arrived yet. The best marketing for a café was a line of people waiting to get in—though the line couldn't be so long that it put people off.

She was packing one of the big glass jars with freshly baked salted caramel and pecan cookies. She looked up again. And then again. But in the end she had to admit to herself she wasn't looking for early customers peering through the plate-glass windows. She was looking for Jesse.

Jesse, who had taken off to Sydney on Sunday, telling her he wouldn't be back until Wednesday evening.

One part of her was upset he would go to Sydney just days before the café was due to open. Another part of her knew she had no right to expect him to be there to help her with all those last-minute things. Especially when she had told him in no uncertain terms she would never want to date him. Both Sandy and Ben had been there after hours to help instead.

Of course the kisses on the beach had changed things between them. How could they not? The kisses at the wedding had been with a hot guy she scarcely knew. But the beach kisses had been with her friend Jesse, a man she'd got to like and in whose company she felt at ease. His kisses had been sensuous, exciting, arousing—but, more than that, it had felt somehow *right* to be sharing such pleasure with Jesse. In spite of all the strikes against him.

She missed him. She missed him more than she could have imagined. She missed his laugh, she missed his manly way of getting things done, most of all she missed that wonderful feeling of being in his arms. Had she been mistaken about him?

She thought about what she'd said to him on the beach, when she'd tried to be honest, but had succeeded only in wounding him— she'd seen the hurt in his eyes. Was she wrong in filing him under P for Player, with a sub-category of H for Heartbreaker? Had she misjudged him? After all, she still didn't know him that well. But what she'd got to know she liked. Liked a lot.

Her caution stemmed from his reputation. But surely her own sister wouldn't have warned her against him if there hadn't been something to be cautious about?

She'd met Philippe when she was twenty-one and had only had one serious boyfriend before him and none after him. Truth was, she didn't have a lot of man mileage on the clock and not a lot of experience on which to make judgements.

Delicious smells wafted into the café, reminding her she needed to be back in that kitchen. Tension was mounting. There had been raised voices, tears, the odd thrown utensil but now all was calm efficiency again.

By seven-twenty a.m. there was a line-up outside the door. By seven forty-five she was so run off her feet she didn't have time to worry about missing Jesse. By eight-thirty young Nikki was in such a fluster managing the constant orders for coffee, Lizzie could see customers tapping impatiently on table tops waiting for their cappuccino, skinny lattes, flat whites and so on. Nightmare!

As she plated an order for French toast with caramelised bananas and blueberries she tried to think what to do. Ask Sandy if she could borrow another waitress from the Hotel Harbourside? Make coffees herself? She'd run through the machine a few times to familiarise herself with it and could probably churn out a halfway acceptable beverage.

Whatever she did, she had to keep calm— if she didn't the whole place would fall apart. She'd have to expect teething problems, Jesse had said. But paying customers were harsh critics. A café would live or die on the reputation of its coffee—if she didn't fix the coffee problem Bay Bites would be going backwards on its first day.

Then, at eight thirty-five, Jesse was there. In the kitchen beside her, tying on his blue-striped apron, joking to the staff that he'd be in trouble with the boss for being tardy.

Her breath caught in her throat and her heart started to hammer so fast she felt giddy. *Jesse.* She ached to throw her arms around him and tell him how glad she was to see him. How she'd felt as though part of her was missing when he wasn't here. But that couldn't happen. They were friends. And he was talking to her as if she were the boss and he was the volunteer helper who was late for work. As it should be, of course. She swallowed down hard on a wave of irrational disappointment.

'I got caught up so couldn't get here until now,' he explained with nothing more than courtesy.

She didn't care where he'd been, just so long as he was with her now. She forced her voice to sound professional and boss-like. 'I'm so glad you're here. Nikki isn't coping with the coffee. If I can ask—'

'I'll take over the coffee machine.'

'What do you mean? How can you do that?'

'I worked a coffee machine when I was a student. Got quite good at it.'

'You didn't tell me.'

'Thought I'd be too rusty to be of any use to you. While I was in Sydney I did a barista course to get me up to speed.'

'You *what?*'

He pulled out a folded up sheet of paper from one pocket then a glasses case from the other. He put on black-framed glasses and unfolded the paper. 'It's a certificate proving I'm officially accredited as a barista. Turns out since I last did this, I first had to do a course in kitchen hygiene so I've got that qualification there too.' He added the last sentence in his mock modest, self-deprecating way she liked so much.

Lizzie didn't know what shocked her most—the fact Jesse had gone to Sydney to train as a barista or how hot he looked in glasses. It added a whole extra layer of hotness to his appeal—not that he actually needed any extra layers.

She lowered her voice so the chef and the kitchen hand who were working nearby couldn't overhear her. 'Why did you do it?'

'I knew you were worried about Nikki. I wanted to help. But I wanted to make sure I wouldn't be more hindrance than help if I'd forgotten how to froth the milk. Turns out I hadn't. And I got a good score for my coffee art, too.'

She stared at him. 'You can do coffee art?'

'Rosettes, hearts. I need some more practice to do a dolphin but I'll get there,' he said, deadpan.

'I'm seriously impressed,' she said. *He'd done it for her and her heart skipped a beat at the thought.*

'It's just steamed milk on espresso, not difficult really.'

As a chef, she knew presentation was a big part of customer appreciation. These days, people had very high expectations of their coffee; they wanted it to look good as well as taste good.

'There's more than that to it; I didn't know you were an artist.' Then she remembered he'd studied art in high school. She was beginning to realise she still had a lot to learn about Jesse. What other surprises were waiting to be discovered?

He shrugged and then winced. 'Your shoulder? What did the doctor say?' she asked.

'It's healing much better than expected,' he said. 'I can probably go back to work soon.'

Her heart plummeted to the level of her clogs.

'That's good,' she said, forcing her voice to be level.

At the back of her mind she'd thought she'd at least have a few more weeks with him around. But there was no time to ask what he intended to do. It would have to wait. Even in the few minutes she'd been speaking to him the orders were piling up.

Jesse got down to business. 'Give Nikki a break from the coffee machine. I'll take over.

Let her wait tables. Later I'll spend some time training her and we'll see if she's good enough to stay.'

Lizzie was too darn grateful that Jesse was back to ask him if he was only going to be there for the two hours he'd defined as his time with her.

The last thing Jesse had thought he'd ever be doing again was making coffee for customers. He was a highly regarded engineer, considered an expert in the quick construction of mass pre-fabricated housing, who had a major corporation jockeying for his skills. He'd had a teleconference with the CEO of the company while he was in Sydney and again they had expressed their keenness in having him on board. They were, in fact, pressuring him to make a decision.

But he also wanted to prove to Lizzie he was not the shallow womaniser she seemed to believe he was. The player label she'd been only too ready to tag him with was really beginning to irk him.

The gratitude and relief on Lizzie's face when he'd told her about the barista course was enough to justify his decision. He'd sensed there'd be trouble with Nikki and had taken the steps that would enable him to help Lizzie achieve her aim of a wrinkle-free launch.

But he'd missed her while he'd been in Sydney. Missed her so much his future—be it in Texas or Asia or wherever he might end up— had seemed somehow bleak without her in it in some way. Never had a hotel room seemed so lonely. The way he'd felt raised questions he wasn't sure of the answers to. He forced himself not to think about it and focused his attention on making coffee.

Flat white, cappuccino, espresso, soy latte, decaf—the orders kept on coming and he kept on filling them. He knew half the customers and had to put up with a lot of good-natured banter.

His answer to the inevitable, 'Hey, Jesse, why the new career path?' was always, 'To help out Sandy and Ben while I'm on leave.'

No way would he admit to anyone that he was doing it with the aim of proving to Lizzie that he was not the guy she thought he was.

But there were customers he didn't know too, total strangers who'd found their way to Bay Bites. People with no connection to the family would be the lifeblood of the new business. Those and the tourists who would eat here a few times, recommend it to their friends, come back next time. He'd noticed lots of empty plates and contented faces. He'd also seen customers photographing their meals with their phones. Free Wi-Fi in the café would pretty much guarantee there would be online reviews up by evening.

He looked up to see Evie's redhead friend he'd met at the taste-test had settled herself at a table and was perusing a menu. She caught his eye and waved. What was her name? Dell, that was right, Dell.

She came up to the counter to say hello. 'Nothing like a handsome barista to bring in business,' she said with her easy, friendly manner.

He smiled. 'I'm also on the front line if they don't like the coffee. But I haven't had any thrown back at me yet.'

Dell smiled back. 'So far, so good, huh? The menu is impressive.'

'All Lizzie's work; I'm just the help.'

'Evie told me Lizzie is a chef who worked in some top restaurants in France and then in Sydney too.'

'That's true,' he said. 'She's highly regarded and has won all sorts of awards.' He felt a swell of unexpected pride in recounting Lizzie's achievements.

'So what brings her to Dolphin Bay?'

'Family,' he said firmly. He was protective

of Lizzie's personal life when it came to discussing it with strangers. No one needed to know about her broken marriage, her ongoing custody issues. *The Morgans looked after their own.*

Dell nodded. 'I hope it all goes well for her.'

Just then Lizzie came out of the kitchen. Immediately Jesse felt her gaze go from him to Dell and back to him. Was that jealousy he saw glinting in her narrowed grey eyes? If so, there wasn't much he could do about it but reassure her she had nothing to worry about. Women liked him. He liked women. But he was not flirting with this girl. And Dell was certainly not sending off any flirty vibes. How could he let Lizzie know that?

He beckoned Lizzie over and introduced her to Dell. 'Dell's been saying some very nice things about the menu.'

'Yes,' said Dell with a friendly smile 'I was at your taste-test party on Saturday. Everything I tried was superb. Kudos to you.'

'Thank you,' said Lizzie.

'And I was saying to your boyfriend that every café needs a handsome barista.'

Lizzie flushed. 'Jesse's not my—'

'We're friends,' Jesse was quick to say. 'Just friends.'

'My mistake,' said Dell. 'I thought… Anyway, I'd better get back to my table and stop holding you guys up. It looks busy.'

'Nothing the kitchen can't handle,' said Lizzie a little stiffly.

Dell rewarded her with a big smile. 'I'm looking forward to my lunch. Congratulations, the café is awesome. I'll bring my guy with me next time; I know he'll love it too.'

Now, at last, Lizzie smiled back. Jesse was puzzled by her sudden change of attitude. Was this some kind of girl talk he wasn't privy too? Had Dell given her a secret semaphore message to make her thaw?

Whatever, he didn't have time to worry about it as the lunchtime coffee orders stepped up. He had worked way more than his allocated two hours but who was counting?

CHAPTER NINE

LIZZIE DIDN'T KNOW how she could thank Jesse enough for what he'd done. To train as a barista just to help her out wasn't something she'd ever imagined Jesse would do. It had caused a radical shift in her opinion of him.

'You saved the day,' she said as they shut up shop at four p.m. Everyone else had gone home and they were the last two remaining in the café, empty now but somehow still echoing with the energy of all the meals cooked, eaten and enjoyed. Bay Bites had been well and truly launched. They'd even sold two paintings. She looked up at Jesse. 'Did I tell you how much I appreciate what you did?'

'Only about a gazillion times, but you can say it again if you like,' he said with the laid-back smile that had appealed to her from the get-go.

'So here's my "thank you number gazillion and one",' she said. 'No matter how good a job we did with the food, our opening day would have been a fail if we hadn't had good coffee.'

'It was far from a fail, Lizzie,' Jesse said. 'I think you can chalk up your first day as a success.'

'Don't say that,' she said quickly. 'We don't want to jinx ourselves.'

He quirked a dark eyebrow. 'I didn't put you down as superstitious.'

'You know how theatre people are full of superstitions? So are restaurant people. No one would be surprised if I had the building blessed, maybe brought in a feng-shui expert. Or burned sage to get rid of any bad karma from the previous business on this site. Maybe even hung crystals in strategic places. And don't even think about whistling in the kitchen. Especially a French kitchen.'

'You're kidding me?'

She shook her head. 'A lot happens in restaurants. First dates. Break-ups. Celebrations. Illicit liaisons. They leave energy. We want good energy. Opening day of a new restaurant is rather like the opening night of a new play. The cast. The audience. The need to have butts on seats. So let's just say I'm cautiously optimistic about how today went and leave it at that.'

He laughed. 'Okay, I'll grant you that. But I still say—'

Lizzie swiped her thumb and first finger across her lips to zip it. 'Don't say it or I'll blame you if anything goes wrong.'

Jesse pretended to cower. Lizzie laughed and ushered him through the back door to the car park. She punched in the alarm code, followed him out and locked the door behind them.

For the first time an awkward silence fell between them. The door that led upstairs to her apartment was only a few metres to the left. Did she invite him upstairs? Be alone with him again? She hadn't been able to stop thinking about how exciting his kisses had been. How much she'd missed him. How maybe she had misjudged him. Would it be wise?

She gestured to the door. 'I can offer you a coffee but I suspect that might be the last thing you want to face right now.'

'I wouldn't say no to a beer,' he said.

'I've got some in the fridge upstairs. I could do with one too.' She gave a sigh that was halfway to a moan of exhaustion. 'There's nothing I want to do more than take off these clogs and kick back.'

The apartment over the café was compact but Sandy had done a wonderful job of refurbishing it for her and Amy. With polished wooden floors throughout, it had been painted in muted neutral tones with white shutters at the windows. Furniture comprised simple, comfortable pieces in whitewashed timber and a plump sofa and easy chairs upholstered in natural linen. The living room window framed a magnificent view of the harbour. The effect was contemporary but cosy and Lizzie's heart lifted every time she came through the door.

'You've settled in,' Jesse said as he followed her through to the small but well-equipped kitchen.

'I just need to get a few more personal touches in place before Amy gets here. Is it "thank you number gazillion and two" if I say how much I appreciate the work you did here?' she said. 'Sandy told me how much of this place is due to your efforts.'

'Enough with the grovelling,' he said with a grin. 'Just get me that beer.'

Lizzie grabbed two beers from the fridge and cut lime quarters to press into the bottle necks. She handed one to Jesse and carried her own through into the living room. 'No food to offer you, I'm afraid,' she said. 'It's all downstairs.'

'I've been snacking on stuff all day,' Jesse said. 'I don't need any more. How do you stay so slim working with all that delicious food?' He cast an appreciative eye over her figure.

'I learned early on to only have very small servings—just tastes really. Then there's the fact that cooking is hard physical work. I'm standing all day every day.'

She flopped down onto the sofa and kicked off her clogs. 'My feet are killing me. They're always killing me. My feet, my knees, my back. It's so good to sit down.'

She wiggled her toes, rotated her ankles, but it didn't do much to ease the deep, throbbing ache in her feet. Damaged feet were an occupational hazard of being a chef.

Jesse sat down on the sofa next to her. 'Let me rub your feet for you.'

Lizzie's gaze met his and there was a question in his eyes that asked so much more than she knew how to answer.

She knew saying yes to his suggestion would be going beyond the bounds of their tentative friendship. But she longed to have his strong, capable hands on her feet, stroking and massaging to ease the pain. Stop kidding herself: she longed to have his hands on her body, full stop. She had gone beyond denying her attraction to him. But was this foot massage a good idea?

'There's some peppermint lotion in the

fridge,' she said. 'It's more soothing when it's chilled.'

Jesse returned from the kitchen with the peppermint lotion. He sat down on the sofa again, put the container on the coffee table. 'Swivel around on the sofa and put your feet across my legs.'

It seemed an intimate way to start a foot massage but she didn't protest. The alternative was to have him kneeling at her feet and that wouldn't do.

Her feet were so sore that Jesse's first firm, sure strokes were painful and she yelped. 'Just getting the knots out,' he explained. He then settled into an easier rhythm, probing, stroking, squeezing with his strong fingers and thumbs, smoothing in the cool, sharply scented lotion.

She moaned her pleasure and relief. 'This is heaven, absolute heaven. Where did you learn to massage like this?'

'Nowhere,' he said. 'I'm just giving you what you seem to need.'

'Oh,' she said, not meeting his gaze.

She didn't know what to say to that. What she did know was she had to keep thoughts of other needs, and the way Jesse might meet them, on a very tight rein.

Her whole body thrummed with the pleasure of what his hands were doing to her heels, toes, soles. She'd never thought of feet as sensual zones but what Jesse was doing was nothing short of bliss.

'I'm just going to lie back and enjoy every minute,' she said, settling further back into the cushions, shifting her feet to fit more comfortably on his thighs.

'You do that,' he said in that deep, resonant voice that had become so familiar. Everything was beautiful about Jesse. His face. His voice. His hands—especially his hands. She moaned again as he massaged the pain away so that now his touch brought only pleasure.

She closed her eyes, zoned out into another world that focused on the rhythmical stroking of Jesse's hands on her feet; the scent of peppermint mingled with the faint aroma of coffee that clung to him; the sound of their breathing, his strong and steady, hers becoming slower, calmer. She could hear the tick, tick, tick of the kitchen clock in the silence of the apartment. *Please don't stop—don't ever stop.*

Eventually, when her feet felt utterly boneless, he finished by stretching out her toes one by one, squeezing her feet one final time, then stroking right up to her shins. 'Done,' he said.

'Mmm…' she murmured as she drowsily sat up, swinging her feet away so she sat near him on the sofa. He might have been massaging her feet but her entire body felt relaxed. 'You're a man of many talents, Jesse Morgan. I guess that's "thank you number gazillion and three". I…'

Her voice got lost in her throat at the intensity of Jesse's expression. She gazed into his face for a long moment, those incredible blue eyes fringed with black lashes, the dark eyebrows, his chiselled mouth. She knew she shouldn't use the word 'beautiful' to describe a man but there wasn't another word that worked as well. Handsome. Good-looking. Striking. He was more than all of those combined. A wave of intense longing for him surged through her.

Now was her chance to move away. To get off the sofa and make an excuse to go into another room. Even to yawn in an exaggerated manner and tell him she needed her beauty sleep and it was time for him to go home.

But she didn't. Instead she reached out her hand and explored his face with her fingers, stroking the tousled hair from his forehead, tracing the line of his thick brows, the ridge of his sculptured cheekbones, the roughness of the dark shadow of his beard, until she reached his mouth. His lips were smooth and warm, the top one slightly narrower than the bottom. His eyes stayed locked on hers. He caught her fingers with his strong white teeth, nipped them gently and she gasped at the unexpected pleasure-pain.

She leaned forward and caressed his mouth with hers. His lips parted under hers and she gave herself over to the sensation of lips, tongue, taste in a slow, easy tender kiss. When he pulled her to him she sank into the embrace of his strong arms around her.

But what had started as gentle rapidly deepened into something more passionate, more demanding that had her winding her fingers through his hair to bring him closer, pressing her body to his hard strength, her heart hammering.

She had been so long without the touch of a man, of skin on skin, the heady delight of breathing in a man's scent. And this was Jesse, who she liked so much, who she was growing to trust, who had appealed to her from the get-go. She wanted so badly to be close to him.

They were alone in the apartment. Anything could happen. But it shouldn't. Not now. Not yet. Sex too soon with Jesse was not a good idea.

She harnessed all the willpower she could muster and pulled away from him. 'That…that wasn't a friend kiss,' she said when she got her breath back.

'No. No, it wasn't,' he said, his voice husky, his breath ragged. 'I like you as much more than a friend, Lizzie. I'd be lying if I said otherwise.'

She shifted a little further away from him on the sofa. With their thighs touching she found it difficult to keep her thoughts straight. 'Me too. I mean…there was a spark between us at the wedding. Now it…it's grown.'

'We got off onto a bad start with each other. You thought I was a guy who picked up and then discarded women just because I could.'

'And you thought I was a…I don't know what you thought I was. Someone too quick to jump to the wrong conclusion?'

'Someone who's trying so hard to protect herself she might not see what could be there,' he said.

She paused to let the implication of his words sink in. 'Perhaps,' she said.

'You seem to have a distorted idea of who I am based on gossip and innuendo. I want to prove to you I'm a decent guy.'

Again she realised that some of her reactions to him might have hurt him. She hastened to reassure him. 'You've shown me that in so many ways. The fact you went off and trained to be a barista just to help me is the latest example.' She looked away and then back. 'It's just…just the other women thing.'

Jesse sighed. She didn't like the sound of it. 'I saw the way you watched me as I talked to Evie's friend.'

'Dell.'

'Were you jealous?'

'A…a little. She's very attractive.'

'Is she? I didn't notice. She's friendly, pleasant.'

'How could you not see how cute she is?'

'Contrary to that bad old reputation of mine, I don't look with lust at every female I meet because I want to bed her and run.'

She managed a weak smile. 'I never thought that for a minute.' Though she'd certainly been told that was what Jesse was capable of. She was beginning to realise the gossips had got him wrong.

Jesse shifted on the sofa, a movement that brought him closer to her. 'I haven't spent much time in Dolphin Bay in recent years. I don't like people knowing my business. It's suited me to let them think Jesse the player has waltzed through life unscathed. If I'd brought Camilla home to marry her it would have been a triumph. But when it turned out such a disaster I was glad I'd never mentioned her. I

didn't want anyone to know I'd been brought
down so low.'

Lizzie was shocked at the slight edge to his
voice. 'Camilla?' she asked.

'She was a photojournalist who came to do
a feature story on our team. We were rebuilding tsunami-ravaged villages in Sri Lanka a
few years back. I wasn't attracted to her at first
but she singled me out for a lot of one-on-one
photography.'

'I bet she did,' Lizzie murmured under her
breath.

'What was that?' asked Jesse.

'Nothing,' she said and decided to keep her
comments to herself. She couldn't be jealous
of someone in Jesse's past and it sounded petty
to criticise the unknown woman.

'I spent a lot of time with her being inter-
viewed, being photographed.'

'And you fell for her.'

'Hard and fast.'

Lizzie jumped down hard on an unwarranted twinge of jealousy. Her imagination was
running crazy wondering what kind of photos
Camilla had taken of Jesse and whether he'd
been wearing any clothes. But she couldn't ask.

'Her time with us was limited,' Jesse continued. 'It was a pressure cooker environment. I

managed to get hold of a sapphire ring. I proposed. She laughed. Then turned me down.'

'She *laughed?*' Indignation for Jesse swept through Lizzie.

'Seemed what I'd thought was a serious relationship was a casual fling to her. She already had a fiancé at home in London. That was the first I'd heard of him. She had never told me she was anything other than single.' The delivery of his words was matter-of-fact, emotionless, as if he didn't care. But the rigid line of his mouth told Lizzie otherwise.

'You must have been devastated.'

He shrugged. 'You could say that.'

'So what happened?'

'She went home to London to marry the poor sucker.'

'And you never saw her again?'

He paused. 'Not from choice.'

'What…what do you mean?'

'She showed up in India at the start of this year to do a follow-up feature.'

'On you?'

'On the organisation I worked for. I wanted nothing to do with her.'

Something about the tone of his voice made her ask, 'But she wanted you?'

'To take up where we left off. Another fling.

She was married by then and prepared to betray her husband.'

Under her breath, Lizzie uttered some choice swear words in French.

'I don't dare ask what that meant,' Jesse said with a shadow of his grin.

'Don't,' said Lizzie.

'Probably nothing I wouldn't have said myself,' he said. 'I told her what I thought of her and got transferred to another site.'

Lizzie put her hand on his arm. 'I hate her on your behalf,' she said vehemently. 'How dare she do that to you? And what an idiot to… to have let you go. I would have…' Her voice tapered off as she realised what she had said. What she had revealed. 'I…I mean—'

Jesse cradled her face in his hands, dropped a kiss on her mouth. 'That's sweet of you,' he said.

She managed a weak smile. 'I…I think you're kinda wonderful. I can't imagine every other woman wouldn't think so too.'

'I'm glad you think I'm wonderful.' He rolled his eyes in self-mockery.

'You…you must know I do. I don't mean that as a joke.'

Her breath hitched with awareness of how attractive she found him but it was so much more than the way he looked. 'I missed you

terribly while you were away in Sydney. It...
it scared me. The thought of what it would be
like when you leave for your job.'

'I missed you too. I thought about you every
minute of that four-hour trip to Sydney and all
the way back.'

He took her hand in his, twined his fingers
through hers. 'So what are we going to do
about it?'

Jesse tightened his grip on Lizzie's hand.
'What's to stop us being more than friends?
From seeing what else we could be to each
other if we gave it a chance. What are the real
issues—issues that can't easily be resolved?
Can we discuss that?' They could beat about
the bush for weeks over this—and he didn't
have weeks.

She answered the pressure of his hand with
hers. 'There's the fact we don't live in the same
country for a start. You seem to be in a different place every few months.'

'That's the nature of my current job.'

'Current? There's something else in the off-
ing?'

'A job that would still involve travel. But I'd
be based in Houston, Texas. That is *if* I choose
to take the job.'

She released her hand from his, smoothed

her hair away from her forehead in a nervous gesture that was becoming familiar. 'Texas is a long way from here. Even further than the Asian countries you seem to work in now. That's a real issue.'

'In the short-term. Long-term, Houston is a good city to live in. With plenty of good restaurants.'

She found her favourite errant lock of hair and twisted it around her finger. 'But there's not just me to consider. There's Amy. She needs stability in her life. She's already been uprooted from France, then from Sydney. And her father still wants her with him every long school vacation. I don't want to disrupt her again.'

'Does it make a huge difference where she lives when she's only five years old?'

Lizzie threw up her hands in an exaggerated shrug. 'I don't know. Maybe. Maybe not. I'm still learning to be Amy's mum. Trying to do my best for her when at times it's been quite difficult. I can't tell you how much I miss her when she's away, like now. But, for her sake, I do everything I can to keep up the relationship with her papa. She loves him and she loves her French grandparents.'

'I can understand that,' he said. That didn't mean he had to like the guy.

Lizzie shifted on the sofa; the movement took her further from him. 'I guess we've already segued into the next issue that might stop us being together—my daughter. Bringing a man into our lives would have ramifications I haven't really thought through. All I know is Amy has to come first.'

'It's not an issue for me,' Jesse said. 'You and Amy come as a package deal and I'm okay with that. We'd have to play it by ear what my role would be with Amy.'

'You know I'm not looking for a father for Amy?'

'I get that.'

'She has a father. Philippe has his faults but he loves his daughter.'

'You said he wants custody?'

'He and his parents want her brought up French. His parents love her too. And she loves her *grand-maman* and *grand-père*. They're wealthy. They think they can give her a good life.'

'Not as good as with her mother.' He felt a fierce surge of protectiveness towards both Lizzie and Amy.

'That's another point I have to consider. Amy is the reason I'm in Dolphin Bay. Thanks to Sandy I've got a job and a home and family nearby. Your mother has said she'll help me with Amy. The local school seems good. I wouldn't give all that up easily.'

'You'd have to weigh up the pros and the cons of another possible change.'

'Yes. That's exactly what I'd have to do.'

He spoke slowly. 'And I have to think about what a possible commitment would mean for me.'

Her quick intake of air told him he'd hit the mark with that one. He knew about the wagers laid on his ongoing bachelor ways. He knew even Sandy called him a 'commitment-phobe'. He wouldn't be surprised if she'd warned her sister off him.

'Did what happened with Camilla make you…make you back away from relationships?' Lizzie asked.

'Yeah. It did. Just when I'd…I'd got over the fire.' Lizzie was the first person he had confided in about Camilla and now this. If he wanted to take their attraction further he owed it to her to be honest.

'The fire that burned down the guest house? When…when you lost Ben's first wife and little boy.'

'It affected us all. We probably should have had trauma counselling. But Morgans don't go in for that. You know what happened to Ben.

He was so deep in despair no one could reach him. Until Sandy came back.'

'Thank heaven,' she said.

'Mum doted on her little grandson. Dad as well. She went extra dotty over dogs after we lost Liam and Jodi.'

'And you?' Lizzie's eyes were warm with compassion.

'I was gutted.'

'But everyone was probably so concerned for Ben they didn't think about the effect on you.'

'And rightly so. But seeing what happened to him made me decide it was never going to happen to me.'

'If you didn't love, you couldn't lose.'

'Something like that. By the time I met Camilla my defences were cracking. I'd realised I had to take my own risks. Make my own way.'

'And then you got hit with Camilla's betrayal.'

'And went backwards.'

Lizzie's smile was shaky at the edges. 'We're quite a pair, aren't we? Both scared of what happened to us in the past happening to us again. Me with Philippe. You with Camilla.'

'I don't know that I'd use the word "scared",' he said.

Jesse thought of the defences he'd thrown

up around the idea of a committed relationship with a woman. The job. The travel. His ongoing career.

Mentally, he pulled himself up. *Stop kidding yourself, mate.*

Work was the wimp excuse. *The wussy versus the brave.* From somewhere deep inside him he had to drag out the truth. At the wedding, he'd felt a real connection to Lizzie that he had never felt before—a connection that had been severed with a painful cut by the way she'd behaved. Now he realised that link could easily fuse together again. *Go further with her and he could get hurt.*

And there was nothing wimpy about avoiding the kind of hurt that could destroy a man. Like the pain he'd felt when Camilla had ended it with him so brutally. Like when Ben had lost his family.

But Ben had found new happiness with Sandy. All around him were people in settled, fulfilling relationships. And he was headed for thirty, older and wiser, he hoped. He realised just telling Lizzie about Camilla's behaviour and hearing Lizzie's outrage on his behalf had done him good.

It had also made him realise how very different the two women were. He doubted that blunt, straightforward Lizzie had it in her to

be as devious as Camilla. What good reason—
what real, valid reason—was there left for him
not to be brave when it came to Lizzie?

'What are we waiting for to happen?' he
asked her. 'If we don't take this chance while
we're actually both in the same country, will
we live to regret it?'

She got up from the sofa, walked across the
room, stood with her back to him for a terri-
fyingly long moment. Then she turned to face
him again, took the steps to bring her closer to
him again. He got up from the sofa to meet her.

'I've had a horrible thought,' she said, still
keeping a distance between them.

'Tell me,' he said, bracing himself for her
words.

She tilted her head to one side. 'What if we
walked away from this and kept up the pretence we were just friends, then the next time
we met was at one of our weddings to someone else?'

A shudder racked him at the thought. 'That
is a horrible thought.'

'Too horrible to contemplate,' she said. 'I
don't know that I could bear it.'

'Me neither. I say we forget the pretence of
friendship. If there's something real between
us then we can address my job, your jealousy
and any other barriers we've put between us.'

She covered the distance between them in a few steps, opened her arms and put them around him. 'Yes,' she said. 'I say yes. We give it a go.'

He drew her tightly to him. This. This was what he wanted.

Lizzie stood close to Jesse in the circle of his arms. She couldn't remember when she'd last felt this mix of happiness and anticipation. Facing the future—even if they were only talking the immediate future—felt so much less scary when she was facing it with Jesse. She could almost feel those barricades she'd put up against him falling down one by one with a noisy clatter.

Her voice was muffled against his shoulder. 'One more thing. There might be a puppy to throw into the mix of things we have to consider.'

He groaned. 'You've been talking to my mother.'

Lizzie pulled away from him so she could look up at his face but stayed in the protective circle of his arms. 'How did you guess?'

'Her house is full of foster dogs and she's always on the lookout for homes for them.'

'Amy would love a puppy. So would I. My

father would never allow us to have pets. I always wanted one.'

'Needless to say, we always had dogs when I was growing up. How could I not love them? I admire Mum for her commitment to rescues.'

'I hear a "however" there,' she said. These days, she picked up on the slightest nuances in his voice.

'Some of the parts of the world I've worked in, children live worse lives than our pampered pooches. It's charities for kids I support.'

Was Jesse saying the things he knew she wanted to hear? She shook her head to rid herself of the thought. She had decided to trust him.

'Are you too good to be true, Jesse Morgan?' she asked.

He shook his head. 'I'm just me, Lizzie— take me as you find me. I didn't tell you that looking for praise,' he said. 'But it's a good way to segue into the fund-raising dinner the dog shelter my mother supports is having on Saturday night.'

'Maura did mention it, so did Sandy. But I said no. I can't afford a late night when I'll have such an early start next day. I'm expecting Sunday to be one of our busiest days at the café.'

'What if you made it an early night?' he

coaxed. 'Just come for the dinner and then I take you straight home?'

Her smile was teasing, mischievous. 'Are you asking me on a date, Jesse?'

'I guess I am. Surely it can't be all work and no play for you.'

'No, but—'

'Where's the "but", Lizzie? You can't use the "just friends" argument any more.'

'I...I don't want everyone in Dolphin Bay knowing our business.' She would never forget that dreadful moment at the wedding when that raucous crowd had discovered her and Jesse kissing on the balcony.

'I understand. And feel the same way. So we keep it private,' he said.

'Even from my sister and your brother?' Sandy was the last person she'd want to know about the change in status of her relationship with Jesse. She didn't want any more warnings or disapproval. Not when she'd decided to switch off her own inner warning system when it came to Jesse.

'If that's what you want,' he said. 'I've never confided in Ben about my relationships.'

'And Amy too, when she gets here on Wednesday. Until...until we know for sure where we're going.' If Jesse were to be a part of her life, they would have to introduce the idea to her daughter with great care.

'Fine by me,' he said.

He cradled her face in his hands. Kissed her briefly, tenderly. Even on that level of kiss, he was a master.

'I'll come to the fund-raiser with you,' she said. 'To everyone there we'll just be friends, but to us—'

'We'll be finding out if we can be so much more.'

'Yes,' she said.

CHAPTER TEN

SATURDAY MORNING WAS so busy at Bay Bites that Lizzie had to call in a casual waitress for extra help. It wasn't just for help with table service; the phone was also ringing off the hook with advance bookings. She was elated and also somewhat surprised that the word had spread so quickly. Don't jinx it, she reminded herself.

She was in the kitchen checking a new batch of the rhubarb and strawberry muffins that had just come out of the oven when Sandy burst in the back door, fizzing with excitement. She grabbed Lizzie by the arm. 'Forget those—they look perfect, smell divine and will probably be gone in ten minutes. Come outside, will you.'

Bemused, Lizzie let herself be dragged outside by her sister. Sandy waved the Saturday edition of Sydney's major newspaper in her face. 'Check this out in the Lifestyle section.

Bay Bites has been included in an article about the foodie scene on the south coast.'

Lizzie felt her stomach plummet to below the level of her clogs. There had already been positive reviews from customers on the internet review sites. But to be reviewed by this newspaper was something different altogether. The review would go on its website too and find its way into prominent positions on search engines. A bad review could seriously damage them at this baby steps stage of the business.

She took hold of the newspaper with shaking hands and focused on the page with some difficulty. The headline was bold and black: *Take the South Coast Gourmet Food Trail.*

She scanned the first paragraphs. They talked about 'the ever-growing food and wine scene', mentioning the lush soil, mild climate, and singling out for praise some of her newly sourced suppliers.

Then there was a list of 'Six Foodie Hotspots' on the south coast. The television chef's restaurant was included. But high on the list was also, to her heart-pounding excitement, Bay Bites.

'Read it out—I've read it ten times already but I want to hear it again,' urged Sandy.

'I…I don't think my voice will work,' Lizzie said.

'Sure it will; come on—read.'

Lizzie cleared her throat and started to read in a voice that started off shaky but gained in strength and confidence as she read:

"'France's loss is the south coast's gain. Talented Aussie chef Lizzie Dumont has returned home to Oz from stints in top restaurants in Lyon and Paris to bring her particular flair to must-visit café Bay Bites in the charming coastal town of Dolphin Bay. The menu is a clever blend of perfectly executed café favourites and more innovative specials that showcase locally sourced ingredients. Don't miss: sublime scrambled eggs; rhubarb and strawberry muffins; slow-cooked lamb with beetroot relish. Then there's the excellent coffee served by the most swoon-worthy barista you'll see this side of Hollywood.'"

The review was accompanied by a photograph of the café interior looking bright and fashionable and another close-up of a muffin broken open with crumbs scattered artfully alongside. Jesse was there beside the coffee machine but his image was blurred, as if in motion, so you couldn't readily identify him.

Lizzie sagged with relief. She looked at the by-line of the journalist who had written such a gratifying review. Adele Hudson. She peered closer at the small photo that accompanied it. She blinked then looked again to make sure she hadn't got it wrong. 'I don't believe it. It's Dell. Adele Hudson is Dell.'

'Who is Dell and how do you know her?' said Sandy.

'She's a friend of Evie from the dairy farm. She was here for the taste-test and then again on our opening day.'

'The redhead flirting with Jesse?'

'Turns out she was interviewing him, in a subtle way,' Lizzie said slowly. She'd thought Dell had been flirting with Jesse too. She felt sick at the memory of the jealousy that had speared her. The review could have gone completely the other way if she'd acted on it.

'Wait. There's more,' she said. 'Adele Hudson is also a well-known food blogger with tens of thousands of followers.'

'Not so well known to us,' said Sandy. She pulled out her e-tablet from her handbag, scrolled through. 'Her blog is called "Dell Dishes". Look, she's written about Bay Bites here, too.'

Lizzie read it out.

'"Good food and good books—two of my greatest loves. I got a taste of both with the newly opened Bay Bites café that's an extension of my favourite south coast bookshop Bay Books."'

She looked up, her excitement rising. 'And

there's so much more about how good the food is. She's picked up on the link between the café and the Hotel Harbourside too and called the hotel restaurant "pub grub at its best".'

'We're on the map now,' said Sandy with a great sigh of satisfaction. 'Along with those five-star ratings on the user review websites, I think we're on our way.' Lizzie laughed as her sister danced her around in a little jig of joy.

'I wondered how word of mouth spread so quickly; we've got a truckload of advance bookings,' said Lizzie. The glowing review certainly took some of the sting out of her demotion in status from fine dining to café cook.

Just then the door from the café opened and the man who had been taking up so much of her thoughts emerged. 'I'm on the hunt for our missing boss,' said Jesse with great exaggeration. He looked from Lizzie to Sandy and back again. His expression grew serious. 'Is something wrong?'

'It's very, very right,' said Lizzie exultantly. She wanted to throw herself into his arms and share with him her excitement and relief.

Sandy rolled her eyes heavenward. 'Better show the review to the "most swoon-worthy barista you'll see this side of Hollywood".'

'What are you talking about?' said Jesse as he grabbed the newspaper. He scanned the pages then groaned loudly and theatrically. 'This will do wonders for my reputation. Please let's hope my mates don't see it.'

'Your handsome face is doing wonders for butts on seats in our café,' said Sandy. 'Would you consider a full-time career change?'

Jesse laughed. 'It's nothing to do with the barista and everything to do with this one.' He swept Lizzie up in his arms and twirled her around. 'Congratulations, boss. You deserve this.'

Now Lizzie felt really elated but as Jesse swung her to a halt she noticed her sister's narrowed, appraising eyes. Sandy's words came back: 'Jesse is so not for you.'

She caught Jesse's eye and, in one of those silent moments of communication they were having more often, he got the message. *Keep Sandy in the dark about us.*

Jesse immediately swung Sandy up and twirled her around too. 'The incredible Adam sisters triumph.'

'I'm a Morgan,' corrected Sandy.

'Dumont for me,' added Lizzie.

Both she and Sandy had been glad to kiss goodbye to their father's name when they'd married. She'd thought of reverting to her maiden name when she'd divorced Philippe but had decided against it for Amy's sake. It had been disruptive enough for her without Mummy having a different name. *Morgan was a nice name.*

She refused to let the thought go further. Anyway, that would be weird. Two sisters marrying a pair of brothers? *Never going to happen.*

CHAPTER ELEVEN

THE STAR OF the fund-raiser for Dolphin Bay Dogs, the shelter Jesse's mother Maura was involved with, was the cast of dogs, ranging from cute puppies to venerable senior citizens with grey around their muzzles.

They sat in a row along the raised platform that acted as a stage for the ballroom of the Hotel Harbourside. The volunteer carers who kept the dogs in check were busy either soothing the nervous ones or calming the excitable ones who just wanted to be part of the action.

It was clever marketing on his mother's part, Jesse thought. He was sure people would be more inclined to open their wallets when they saw those pleading canine eyes.

But, appealing as the puppies were, Jesse's eyes were only for Lizzie. They'd agreed she'd arrive with Sandy and Ben so as not to draw attention to the way their 'friendship' had escalated into something so much more.

And now she was here. As she made her way across the room to him he was literally lost for words. His heart thudded into overdrive and his mouth went dry.

Last time he'd seen her she'd been wearing her chef's jacket and black pants, her hair pulled tightly back from her face and her cheeks all flushed from the heat of the kitchen. He'd thought she'd looked lovely then. But the transformation from chef to seductress was nothing short of sensational.

Her dress clung to her slender shape and left her shoulders bare, with a tantalising suggestion of cleavage, and its colour was a tint of aqua that glistened like the underside of a wave on Silver Gull beach. Her hair puzzled him for a moment until he realised it looked so different because her wild curls had been tamed into a style that was straight and sleek and falling around her face. She looked sophisticated. Elegant. And sexy as all get-out.

'Lizzie,' he said in the most casual just-friends voice he could muster, 'you're looking very lovely.'

'Thank you,' she said in the tone she used to accept a compliment about the food from a customer, but lit by a mischievous sparkle in her eyes. 'So glad you approve.'

'I approve, all right,' he said, his voice more

the hoarse whisper of a lover than the light tone of a pal, no matter how he tried to keep it casual.

The silver high heeled shoes that strapped around her ankles brought her to easy kissing height. She kissed him lightly, first on one cheek and then the other. 'Just friends, remember,' she murmured into his ear.

It was an effort not to clamp her possessively to his side. To beat away anyone who came near her. She aroused caveman instincts he hadn't known he possessed.

'You look so beautiful,' he murmured back. 'No man would want to stop at just being friends.'

She laughed as she pulled away from him to normal conversation level. He had better try and mask the hunger in his eyes.

'I bought this dress in Paris years ago. It's so long since I dressed up I could hardly remember how. I thought it was going to be a big fail.'

'Count it as a first class honours pass,' he said.

She wore make-up too, dark stuff around her eyes that brought out a purple ring around her iris. And deep pink lipstick on her sweet, seductive mouth. It only made him want to kiss it off.

'This is the same room where Sandy and

Ben's wedding reception was held, isn't it?' Lizzie asked in a low murmur. 'Do you get a feeling of déjà vu?'

'In a way,' he said. 'You're the loveliest woman in the room again.'

'I bet you say that to all the girls,' she said in mock flirtation, but he saw a touch of wariness in her eyes.

'No, I don't, and that's the truth,' he said. He bent to whisper in her ear. 'You have to learn to trust me, Lizzie.' *As he had to trust her.*

She nodded. 'I know.'

He wanted to kiss her to reassure her, but of course he couldn't. Not with the eyes of a sizable number of his family and friends upon them.

'One thing is for sure,' she said, as if she'd read his mind. 'Nothing could take me out onto that balcony again.'

He didn't want to share her. Wanted her all to himself somewhere very private. But she was right—that place wasn't the balcony. No matter how beautiful the view of the full moon over the bay.

He was about to tell her that when Ben came up beside them. He slapped his brother on the shoulder in greeting. 'It's not you I've come to talk to,' Ben said. 'It's Lizzie.'

'Okay,' said Lizzie. Did she feel as annoyed as he did at being interrupted?

'Mum wants to show you something special,' Ben said to Lizzie. 'She's over there near the stage. Please don't be surprised if it's a dog.'

Lizzie laughed. 'I don't mind at all if it's a dog. Isn't that what we're here for?'

She casually brushed her hand against Jesse's arm as she left—he got the message she would rather stay with him and it pleased him.

'I actually do want to talk to you,' said Ben. He went from smiling to serious, as he did when money and investment was concerned.

Jesse's interest was sparked. When he was younger, he'd trusted Ben with financial advice that had paid off very handsomely. A generous inheritance plus business savvy and wise investment meant that at his age he was very well off. Well off enough to be able to take the weight right off Lizzie's feet if that was what she wanted; maybe into a job that wasn't so physically demanding. It concerned him to see her so exhausted and in pain at the end of a long day in the kitchen.

'I want to talk to you about a business proposition,' Ben said.

'If you want to hire me as a full-time barista, forget it,' Jesse said with a grin.

'Sandy would sign you up in a moment,' Ben said. 'But that's not the money-making proposal I have for you.'

As Lizzie walked away from Jesse, she was surprised to realise how much she was enjoying herself. She couldn't help but contrast the last time she'd been in this room for Sandy's wedding.

Then she'd been the bride's sister who didn't know anyone. Now, even after only a few weeks in Dolphin Bay, she recognised lots of faces and they were all very complimentary about Bay Bites. Several people told her they'd put in bids for the prize of lunch for two she'd donated to the silent auction.

Maura came bustling up and swept her up into a hug. 'Gorgeous, gorgeous dress,' she said. 'So glad to see you having a night out.'

'We had another busy day in the café today,' Lizzie told her. 'The fish pie I made from your recipe was a sell-out. And we've already got customers asking us to put your strawberry sponge cake on the regular menu.'

'Only serve that cake when strawberries are at their finest,' Maura advised. 'It's at its best with the freshest, sweetest strawberries. Anything else is a compromise and the flavour will suffer.'

Lizzie smiled. Maura truly was a woman after her own heart when it came to food. 'I'll keep that advice in mind,' she said.

'I'm pleased about that, dear. But we're not here to talk about cooking. There's someone I want you to meet.'

Lizzie followed Maura up onto the platform where the dogs were waiting to play their roles for the evening with varying degrees of good behaviour.

'If we can appeal to people's hearts for adoptions tonight that will be grand,' said Maura. 'If we can get them to open their wallets, too, that's all the better.'

Lizzie suppressed a smile. It appeared the Morgan family were born businesspeople. That augured well for the future of Bay Bites—and her own security in Dolphin Bay.

Maura led Lizzie to where a puppy snuggled with a teenage girl. 'He's sad, Mrs Morgan,' she said. 'He misses his brother and sister who got adopted.'

'Sad? Maybe a little lonely,' said Maura. 'But he's quiet because he's exhausted from being run around the yard all afternoon.' She turned to Lizzie. 'Meet Alfie.'

At the sound of his name, the puppy sat up. He was black with a few irregular white patches, soulful dark eyes and long floppy ears that made Lizzie think he had some spaniel in him. He gave a sweet little whine and lifted up a furry paw to be shaken.

Lizzie was smitten. 'Oh, he's adorable.' She shook the puppy's warm little paw.

'Mother, are you up to your "get the puppy to shake paws" tricks again?' Jesse spoke from behind her and Lizzie turned. Her heart missed a beat at the sight of how devastating he looked in a tuxedo. She hadn't thought he could look more handsome than he did in his jeans and T-shirt but he did. Oh, yes, he did.

'And if a few tricks help a homeless animal find his way into someone's heart, who am I to miss the opportunity?' said Maura with the charming smile that was so like her son's.

'He's won my heart already—can I pick him up?' Lizzie asked.

As soon as he was in her arms the puppy tried to enthusiastically lick her face. Lizzie laughed. 'Jesse, isn't he cute?'

'He is that,' said Jesse with a smile she could only describe as indulgent.

'Amy would adore him.'

'Yes, she would,' said Maura. 'A dog can be a great friend to a little girl.'

'Her *grand-maman* in France has a little dog that Amy loves. She's heartbroken every time she says goodbye to her. It might help her to settle here if she had a dog of her own.'

'But is it practical for you to have a puppy?' Jesse asked.

'Not right now,' Lizzie said reluctantly, kissing the puppy's little forehead. 'Who knows what the future might bring for us? But he's utterly enchanting.'

She turned to Maura. 'Amy will be here on Wednesday. If Alfie hasn't found a home by then I'll bring her to see him.' She gave the puppy one more pat, to which he responded with enthusiastic wagging of his tiny tail, and reluctantly handed him back to his carer.

Maura put her hand on Lizzie's arm. 'You have to do what's best for you and your daughter. But a dog brings such rewards.'

If Lizzie stayed in Dolphin Bay a dog would be possible. For one thing, she'd be happier if Amy had the comfort of a puppy while she settled into her new home and made new friends. But it was still early days yet.

It wasn't just the possibility of something serious with Jesse that made her hesitate. She only had a job here if the café was a success. Otherwise she'd be back in Sydney flat-hunting in a difficult rental market with the added hindrance of a dog in tow.

And then there was Jesse's career. If they had a future together, where might it be?

'Don't you have to give your speech soon, Mum?' Jesse said.

'Yes, of course I do,' said Maura. 'You just keep little Alfie in mind, Lizzie.'

Jesse put his arm casually around Lizzie's shoulder as he led her down from the platform. 'Don't let her talk you into something you're not ready for. A dog's a big commitment.'

'Don't I know it,' she said.

She was silent for a long moment. Holding the squirming little bundle in her arms had brought back memories of Amy as a baby. Amy often asked if she could have a little brother or sister, but another baby had never been on the agenda. Why was she thinking about it now?

As the evening progressed Lizzie couldn't help being overwhelmed by that déjà vu. They were in the same room as the wedding reception. She was enjoying the opportunity to wear a beautiful dress, do something special with her hair—she loved the effect of having it straight—and wearing more make-up than usual.

With the Parisian dress she felt she had donned some of her old Lizzie party-girl spirit. That Lizzie had been pretty much smothered by maternal responsibilities and anxieties. She loved Amy more than she could ever have imagined loving another person. But there were times she wanted to be Lizzie, not just Mummy or Chef. This was one of them. She was determined to enjoy every second of the evening.

She even enjoyed the speeches. She wasn't the only one near tears when Maura spoke about the homeless dogs and cats in the area and the maltreatment some of them received before they got to the shelter. Someone else spoke convincingly about spaying and neutering to help bring down the number of unwanted kittens and puppies.

When Maura returned to the table after the speeches, she saw the pride in Jesse's father's eyes as he helped his wife of heaven knew how many years back into her chair. She realised Jesse had been brought up in a family where love and kindness ruled.

How very different from her family, where her father, a specialist anaesthetist, believed in excessive discipline, rigorous academic achievement and ruthless competition. No wonder both she and Sandy had rebelled. No wonder her mother had eventually divorced him and moved to another state.

Her father hadn't been a part of her life for

a long time but he had asked to see her when she'd brought Amy back to Australia. She'd hoped he'd regretted the way he'd treated her, maybe wanted to make up for it by developing a relationship with his granddaughter. But no. He wanted to pay to send Amy to an exclusive girls' boarding school where she could develop her academic potential, away from her mother's influence. Needless to say, Lizzie had declined the offer.

The food at Maura's function was good, but not as good as she'd expected from the Hotel Harbourside catering. 'Should I mention it to Sandy?' she whispered to Jesse. They were seated together at the Morgan family table, surreptitiously holding hands under cover of the tablecloth.

'When the moment is right,' Jesse said, keeping his voice very low, pretending not to be too interested in what she was saying. 'You'll need to be diplomatic.'

'Aren't I always diplomatic?' she started to say in a huff.

He smiled. 'You can't pride yourself on being both blunt and diplomatic at the same time.' He squeezed her hand to emphasise he didn't mean it as an insult.

'Point taken,' she said.

Again she marvelled at how quickly Jesse

had got to know her. She didn't feel she knew him as well but was enjoying each revelation of what lay beneath the heartbreakingly handsome exterior. So far she'd discovered he was a thoughtful, highly intelligent man with a good heart, a good head for business and a whole lot of common sense. That was on top of being a master kisser.

'Do you know what I'm missing?' she said. 'The music. I wish I could get up and dance with you. Do you remember how we danced together at the wedding?'

'How could I forget?'

'I think dancing with you was when I—' She swallowed the words that bubbled to the surface. *When I thought I might have found someone special.*

'When you...?' Jesse prompted.

'When I...when I realised you were so much more than the best man who I, as the chief bridesmaid, was obligated to spend time with.'

And now? *Now she was falling in love with him.* She'd fought it so hard she hadn't let herself recognise it. *Could you fall in love this quickly?*

'You okay?' asked Jesse. 'You seem flustered.'

'Yes. Yes. Of course I'm okay.' *How did she deal with this?*

'I want to dance with you too,' said Jesse in a husky undertone. 'The evening is winding up. In half an hour we leave separately, then—'

'Yes?' she asked, her heart thudding.

'Then we have our own private dance on the beach.'

CHAPTER TWELVE

JESSE WAITED UNTIL a moment when his mother
had got back up onstage and was introducing
the audience to the dogs. She held up a particularly cute puppy with one ear that flopped all
the way over. All attention was on the puppy
as the other guests oohed and aahed at its cute-
ness. He didn't think anyone would notice him
slip away and make his way out of the hotel.

Ten minutes later he saw Lizzie creep out of
the Hotel Harbourside exit and cross the road
to where he waited. For a moment she didn't
see him and her wary look made his heart leap.

He couldn't have anticipated how fast things
were moving with her. But he was a man used
to making quick life-or-death decisions. He
had decided he wanted to take a chance on
Lizzie Dumont—and no obstacle was going to
be allowed to stand in the way of them becoming a couple. That included his own doubts.

She caught sight of him and smiled—a joyous smile tinged with mischief, just like the smile he had fallen for when he had first met her at the pre-wedding outing. She ran over the road to meet him under the palm tree that edged the beach. 'I feel like a naughty schoolgirl sneaking out like this,' she said with a delightful giggle.

Funny, he hadn't been attracted to her when she was a schoolgirl. It was the woman she'd become who'd caught his attention.

'So where's the dance floor?' she asked.

'Down there.' He indicated the beach with an expansive wave of his hand. 'If we dance down there and to the left we'll be out of sight of the hotel.'

Her gasp of pleasure was the biggest reward he could have asked for. 'So we twirl and whirl on the sand,' she said.

She balanced on his shoulder as she leaned down to unbuckle the straps on her silver shoes and slip them off. She tucked them alongside his own shoes, socks and bow tie where he'd discarded them at the base of the palm tree.

'The wet sand near the edge of the water will be firmer,' he said with his engineer's brain.

The full moon was high in the sky and its reflection lit a shimmering path of palest gold from the horizon, over the water to where the tiny waves of the bay sighed onto the sand.

'Magic by moonlight,' she breathed.

It was so light he could clearly see Lizzie's eyes, her face pale, uplifted to the moon, her hair glinting like silver. She looked ethereal, like some kind of fairy princess in her shimmering dress.

Jesse could hardly believe he was thinking such thoughts. He was an engineer. Practical. Mathematical. *Madness* by moonlight, more like it.

She wound her arms around his neck. 'I feel like I'm in some kind of enchanted world,' she whispered. 'And you're the handsome prince spiriting me away to dance on moonbeams. Have I found my way onto the pages of one of Amy's fairy tale books?'

He kissed her, lightly, possessively. 'If that's the case, you're the fairy princess.' *Had he actually said that?*

'I had no idea you were so romantic, Jesse,' she murmured.

'I'm not usually,' he said. 'It…it's you.'

This was the Lizzie who had captivated him at the wedding. During the last ten days he'd got to see the other sides of Lizzie. And the more he got to know her, the more he wanted her in his life.

She laughed and the slightly bawdy edge to her laughter reminded him how utterly real and womanly she was. 'Where's the music, Prince Charming? Can you conjure it up from the moonlight?'

'The prosaic engineer in me would tell you I can play music through my smartphone.'

'Whereas Prince Charming might say we can dance to the music of the stars,' she suggested.

'And the rhythm of the waves,' he said.

'With those chirping crickets adding some bass.'

He laughed. 'If you say so.'

'It's perfect,' she whispered.

She went into his arms and together they danced barefoot on the cool, wet sand with the occasional tiny cold wave swishing over their feet and making her squeal. They danced not with the expertise of ballroom dancers—he'd never mastered that art—but in their own rhythm, making up their steps as they went along, her glittering skirt twirling around them.

'I don't know that the music of the moon and stars is enough; it hasn't quite got a beat,' she murmured. 'Shall I hum? I can't sing, so humming will have to do.'

'Go ahead and hum,' he said, falling more under her spell each minute, totally enchanted by her.

He stood quite still as she started to hum the tune of the old song about Jesse's girl that had tormented him for so many years. But in her slightly tuneless hum, it was the most melodious music he'd ever heard. And her particular version of the words echoed in his heart as she murmured them.

He smoothed her hair back from her face, cupped her face in his hands. 'Do you really want to be Jesse's girl?'

Her eyes were luminous in the moonlight. 'Oh, yes,' she said.

Lizzie pulled Jesse back for another kiss. She couldn't bear to spend a minute out of his arms on this magical evening where her own Prince Charming was dancing her along an enchanted beach. Only too soon her prince might have to go across those waters to the badlands to fight his own battles and maybe never come back to her.

She'd not been one for fairy tales. As a mother, she'd tried to steer Amy in the direction of feminist tales of hard-working women who met men on an equal footing, who had no room for Prince Charmings riding to their rescue on white chargers when they could rescue themselves perfectly well, thank you very much.

But tonight with Jesse she felt differently.

Whether it was indeed the magic of the full moon or because she was falling in love with him, she wanted Jesse to be her prince, sweep her up into his arms and carry her away to make her his.

Even if it was only for tonight she wanted this, wanted him. She lost herself in his kisses, yielding to his lips, to his tongue as his mouth claimed hers, trembled with pleasure at the sensation of his hands on her bare shoulders.

'It's about at this stage Prince Charming sweeps the princess off to his fairy tale castle,' she murmured against his mouth.

Jesse lifted his head to meet her gaze. 'To make her his?'

He had never looked more handsome than at this moment. His hair raven's wing black in the moonlight, his eyes reflecting the indigo of the deep night sea.

'Yes,' she breathed. 'To make her his in every sense of the word.'

'Are you sure?' His voice was deep, husky with a slight hitch that betrayed his fear she might say no.

There was no risk of that. She nodded. 'My Cinderella garret above the café is all mine right now. On Wednesday the junior princess will be in residence. You might find I turn back into a pumpkin then.'

Jesse laughed, his perfect white teeth gleaming in the moonlight. 'I think you're getting your analogies mixed. Even I know it was the carriage that got turned back into a pumpkin. You've left your shoes on the beach. It will be the prince doing the rounds of every house in the magical town of Dolphin Bay trying to find whose foot fits the silver stiletto.'

She smiled. 'So, not a pumpkin. But it's true that at five a.m. I'll turn back into a servant wearing rags and clogs as I stoke the fires of the café kitchen. Well, maybe not rags but—'

He dropped a kiss on her nose. 'The clock is ticking.'

'My castle or yours?' she said.

'As I'm staying in the boathouse, your garret might be more private.'

'My garret it is,' she said.

Laughing, kissing, Jesse danced her over the sand and back up to where they had stashed their shoes. He knelt in the sand and helped her wipe off the sand from her feet. Then he kissed the arch of each foot before he slipped on her silver stilettos.

'I had to stop myself from doing that the night I massaged your feet,' he said.

Delicious ripples of pleasure shimmered through her. 'No need to stop now,' she whispered.

Totally engrossed in the magic of being with Jesse, Lizzie didn't care who might see them make their way hand in hand towards her apartment. There, in true fairy tale prince fashion, he gathered her into his arms and carried her up the stairs and into the magical kingdom of her bedroom.

CHAPTER THIRTEEN

JESSE HAD AGREED with Lizzie to keep secret the new turn their relationship had taken. In the three days since their dance on the beach they'd managed not to arouse suspicion. Neither of them wanted to be subject to the inevitable teasing the revelation they were dating would bring. To him, Lizzie was not just one in a stream of 'Jesse's girls'. As far as he was concerned, she was the one and only Jesse's girl.

This wasn't something short-term. He was convinced of that. Lizzie wasn't underhand and dishonest like Camilla had been. He trusted her.

He intended to talk to her today about the proposition he had discussed in depth with Ben. His brother had suggested they pool some of the land they each owned around Dolphin Bay and form a property development company.

Jesse had been involved in the building of

the Hotel Harbourside and was a part-owner of the new spa resort Ben was building. At the back of his mind he'd always wanted to go into business for himself; he came from a long line of entrepreneurs. It was a logical—and exciting—next step.

Relocating back to Dolphin Bay would also knock down the major barrier that remained between him and Lizzie—that they lived in different countries. It was a move that checked all the boxes. Importantly, it would give them time to really get to know each other.

He'd arranged to meet Lizzie after the café closed for the day. The young waitress Nikki had responded so well to his training and confidence-boosting, he'd done himself out of his job as a barista. His role at Bay Bites now comprised helping out for a few hours over lunchtime—and that was only an excuse to be with Lizzie. His two-hour time limit? Twenty hours of Lizzie's company a day wouldn't be enough.

She was already there when he got to the lookout, a block away from the café, with the best view in Dolphin Bay of the harbour. It was a perfect afternoon, the water sparkling aquamarine under a cloudless sky. Fishing boats and pleasure craft of all shapes and sizes bobbed on the water and the melodic chime of rigging against masts carried across to where he stood.

Lizzie wore a pink sundress that bared her shoulders and arms. Fine tendrils of her pale blonde hair had escaped from the band that held it back from her face and wafted in the slight breeze. There was no reason for her to be anything but happy and relaxed. But he could see straight away that something was bothering her—he'd learned to read the way anxiety tightened her face and dimmed the light in her eyes.

They greeted each other with a discreet kiss on the cheek—as friends, colleagues and family connections would. After a night of lovemaking, he'd left her warm and satisfied in her bed when he'd exited before dawn. It had been difficult to leave her but they both wanted to keep their new intimacy a secret.

'What's up?' he asked.

'How do you always know?' she asked with the shadow of a smile.

'Just observant,' he said.

But it was more than that. The connection between them grew stronger with each minute they spent together. It was a bond he'd never had before. But it also brought fear of the inevitable pain if that connection was ever severed. *Wussy versus brave,* he reminded himself.

He'd chosen to take the brave path, to let feeling grow rather than stifle it with fear. So, it seemed, had she.

Lizzie took his hand and gave it a surreptitious squeeze. He knew without further words being spoken that she valued the depth of their connection too.

She looked up at him 'You know Amy is due back tomorrow?'

'I know how much you're looking forward to seeing her. Why the glum face?'

'Philippe is escorting her on her flight from Lyon. I was going to drive up to Sydney to meet her plane. Now he'll hire a car to bring her here.'

'Your ex? Here in Dolphin Bay?' He was hit by a blow of dismay. Lizzie's ex-husband played an active role in Amy's life. But having him here on home turf was not a move he welcomed.

'It's as much a surprise to me as it is to you,' she said.

For her sake, he suppressed the stab of jealousy that knifed him. 'That's good for Amy.'

'Yes. The airline does a wonderful job of escorting her. In fact she enjoys the fuss the attendants make of her so much she's probably protesting having her papa with her. But

I worry every second she's on the plane by herself so in that way I'm glad he'll be there.'

'Of course you are.'

He admired Lizzie's dedication to her daughter. Amy was a fantastic little kid, smart, funny, outgoing. If—and it was still a big if—he got to be a permanent part of Lizzie's life he would welcome a role in Amy's life too.

'I'm worried about why Philippe wants to see me so much he's flying all the way to Australia.' That favourite stray piece of hair was getting another workout between her fingers.

'Maybe because he's missing you.' Jesse spoke lightly but his gut roiled.

'Nothing like that,' she said, shaking her head with a vehemence Jesse should have found reassuring but didn't. If he'd had Lizzie for his own, he would never have let her get away. Her ex-husband must have regretted it a million times. Maybe that was what he wanted to tell her. Perhaps he had a good story to spin about how he'd changed.

'He says there's something important that has to be said face to face,' Lizzie continued.

The ex wanted her back. Jesse just knew it. 'So what do you think your ex wants?'

'I'm terrified he's going for full custody of Amy. He's used it as a threat before to try and keep me in France. I can't think what else he would need to see me about.'

Jesse thought he knew only too well what her ex would want: Lizzie and Amy back with him. But he didn't share his thoughts. Instead he reassured her. 'You're a wonderful mother. You can provide a secure home for Amy. No way would he have grounds to say you're unfit for custody. Don't the courts usually rule in favour of the mother?'

Lizzie snatched her hand to her mouth. 'The courts? Please don't let it get that far.'

'You'll know tomorrow what he wants. There's nothing you can do in the meantime. Try to stop worrying.' He didn't want her to be preoccupied with her ex on the last night they had together alone before Amy came home. The dynamic between them would be changed when they had to fit their private time around the needs of a five-year-old.

'If their flight is on time and all goes well, he and Amy should be here by midmorning.'

She banged the railing of the seafront wall with such force it surely must have hurt her hand. 'Why is he doing this to me? After all he put me through before? I've done everything I can to be civilised about the divorce, to make it easier for Amy. Letting her go to France half of every school holidays. Video calls every week.

Why?' She muttered under her breath in what Jesse could only assume was a string of fluent French swear words.

It was the closest to anger he had seen her, though he'd heard a few explosions coming from the kitchen at Bay Bites. 'You really don't want to see him, do you?'

'Of course I don't. Why would I?'

Jesse's spirits lifted at the thought. Sounded as if any possible reunion could be wishful thinking on the ex-husband's part.

'Do you want me to be there when you meet with him?'

'No.'

Her answer came with such swiftness that Jesse felt as if he'd been hit with an unexpected punch between the eyes. 'Whatever,' he said.

Her face filled with contrition. She reached out and touched him fleetingly on the cheek with slender, cool fingers. 'I didn't mean to sound hurtful. Of course I would like you by my side when I confront Philippe. But if he's after sole custody, I wouldn't want him to know I was in a relationship with a man.'

'I don't want to jeopardise anything,' Jesse said. 'But I'll be at hand. Just in case.'

'No need for that,' she said. 'Philippe hasn't got a violent bone in his body. I wouldn't let Amy spend so much time with him if he had any tendencies that way. No. I can handle this by myself—like I did with the issues that ended the marriage.'

Jesse muttered assent. But no way would he let Lizzie go into this by herself. When she met with her ex he would be nearby.

But, to help her, he needed to know what had happened to end the marriage in such a drastic way she'd come back to Australia to raise her child on her own.

'Lizzie, we've skirted around this. But what actually happened to end your marriage? To make you so wary of men like your ex.'

Lizzie hated reliving the past. She and her sister had handled what had happened with their father by having a 'water under the bridge' policy that had so far served her well.

But Jesse deserved to know.

'I don't really like to talk about this, so I won't linger on the details,' she said.

'Fine by me,' he said. He leaned back against the lookout wall with his back to the view. Lizzie couldn't help thinking she'd rather look at Jesse than any number of rustic stone breakwaters and charming boats in the harbour, no matter how picturesque.

'I met Philippe when we were both working at a hotel up in Port Douglas. When he left to go back home to France I went with him. It was an adventure—and good for my career. Living in Paris was a ball, working all hours then partying hard.'

'I hear a "but" coming on.'

She nodded. 'I fell pregnant. It was unplanned. But we got married, made the best of it. When there were some complications in the pregnancy, I wanted to go home to have the baby. My French had improved out of sight by then but I didn't feel I really understood the doctors and the hospitals. Philippe didn't much like it—and his family were horrified—but I came home to stay with Sandy.'

'Why didn't your husband go with you?'

'He had a really good job; I didn't want him to give it up. Not when we were about to have a child to support. Neither of us wanted to accept money from his parents with the strings that went with it.'

'I wouldn't have let you go by yourself. Under any circumstances.'

'You're you. Philippe was Philippe.' She looked up at Jesse. 'I really, really hate talking about this.'

'I wish I could hug you but, in case you hadn't noticed, a couple of my mother's friends are walking on the other side of the road. If I touch you, the whole town will soon know.'

Lizzie turned around. Sure enough, two older ladies who had become regulars at the café and drank more cups of tea in the space of an hour than she had imagined anyone could possibly drink, had drawn level to them. She forced a smile and waved to them.

She turned back to Jesse. 'I see what you mean. I want to hug you too. More than you could know. But I'll get on with the story so I can be done with it.' She gritted her teeth. 'I got back to France and knew immediately something was different.'

'To cut a long story even shorter, he'd met someone else,' said Jesse with a scowl.

'How did you know that?'

'Lucky guess,' he said.

He must dislike hearing this as much as she disliked saying it. She appreciated how difficult it must have been for him to tell her about that dreadful Camilla.

'She was a *commis,* a junior chef, in the restaurant where Philippe worked. He said it meant nothing.'

'He was lonely; she threw herself at him,' Jesse drawled, contempt edging his voice.

'All that. He confessed and begged my forgiveness.'

Jesse's mouth tightened to a thin line. 'You

know my opinion. No cheating under any circumstances.'

Was Jesse judging her? She wished she hadn't started this conversation.

'What choice did I have? I was twenty-three, had a brand new baby. We moved to Lyon to make a fresh start. I went back to work when Amy was six months old. But things were very different. No more party girl Lizzie.'

'I think I can predict the rest.' Jesse's hands were curled into fists.

'He swore he was faithful but I couldn't believe him. I was so jealous and suspicious I became a horrible person no one would want to live with. I stuck it until Amy was four. You know the rest.'

'Did you love him?' Jesse's question came from left field.

'I thought I did.'

'What do you feel about him now?' Jesse's voice was tight, his eyes guarded.

She frowned. 'That's a strange question to ask after what I've been telling you. Philippe is done and dusted as far as I'm concerned. Not only do I not love him, I don't actually like him.'

Jesse's face darkened. 'Best I don't meet the guy tomorrow. You might not be able to hold me back.'

'I've probably said too much. But now you know why I resisted getting involved with someone I thought might hurt me in the same way.'

CHAPTER FOURTEEN

THE NEXT DAY Lizzie was so nervous about the upcoming confrontation with Philippe she felt nauseous. She had organised extra help in the kitchen so she could spend the day with Amy. That also allowed her time for a private meeting with her ex-husband. Dread that he might try to take Amy away from her put her so on edge she wasn't fit to work anyway.

In the fairy tale her life in Dolphin Bay with Jesse had become, she cast Philippe in the role of the ogre who could take her happiness away. She was ready with sword and shield to fight him. She had given up her career and moved to Dolphin Bay for Amy's sake. She could give her daughter a good life here. She would never, ever let her go.

The reunion with Amy had been ecstatic, as it always was when they'd been apart for any length of time. She'd held her darling girl tightly to her, breathed in the apple shampoo freshness of her, laughed and pretended to squirm at Amy's exuberant hugs and kisses.

As usual after Amy had been with her father and his family it had taken her a few minutes to adjust to speaking English, to being a little Australian girl again. But after Lizzie had shown her the café—where the staff had made a huge fuss of her—and her new home upstairs, Amy had happily gone off with Maura. No doubt she would be introduced to little Alfie and then the begging and pleading to keep him would start. Lizzie decided to keep an open mind on that one.

Maura had so much grandmotherly love to give—and Amy was the only child in their family she had to lavish it on. Lizzie was aware of the thread of sadness underlying Maura's warmth, stemming from the tragic loss of Ben's little son.

With Amy settled with Maura, now it would be just her and Philippe, squaring up against each other as adversaries with their child the spoils of battle. She hadn't seen her ex-husband for more than a year. Sometimes she liked to imagine he didn't exist. But he was here in Dolphin Bay. She took a deep steadying breath to centre herself and headed to the Hotel Harbourside. *Let the battle begin.*

She'd chosen neutral territory, a quiet corner

of the guest lounge. At this time of day, during the week, there should be no one to disturb them. She regretted the hurt that had flashed across Jesse's face when she had declined his offer to accompany her. But this was something she had to do by herself.

She cast a quick eye around the room. Jesse had said he would be nearby in case he needed to rush in to her defence—like a true Prince Charming would. She couldn't see him anywhere, but she trusted he was there. Jesse was true to his word. Although she knew the confrontation with Philippe wouldn't get physical—unless he'd changed out of sight—it was reassuring to know that Jesse was close.

Then Philippe was there, greeting her with his accented English that had charmed her years ago. She braced herself and looked up at her ex, his handsome face with his prominent nose and Amy's eyes, his dark blond hair. He had once been so dear to her; they had started off with such high hopes, now he meant nothing. There was an element of sadness—of failure—to her thoughts but no regret. If it wasn't for Amy, she would be happy never to have to see him again.

Jesse knew the layout of the Hotel Harbourside very well. It had not been difficult to find a spot where, with the help of a large wall mirror, he could sit in a large, high-backed lounge chair and keep an eye on Lizzie without her—or her ex-husband—seeing him. He held an open newspaper in front of him and flicked through its pages without seeing a word. It was like a stake-out. Cloak and dagger stuff. Only this was a game where the stakes were very high.

Lizzie had come into the guest lounge by herself. She was dressed more formally than he had seen her, wearing narrow black trousers and a tight cropped jacket with the sleeves pushed up. Her hair was pulled back in a thick plait that hung in pale contrast down the back of the black jacket. She looked elegant, stylish and so unfamiliar it disconcerted him.

He could tell by the way Lizzie squared her shoulders and measured her stride that she was nervous. Was that why she had dressed like that? As armour? The ugly thought intruded. Or to look good for her ex?

She only had seconds to pace the floor by herself before she was joined by a tall guy wearing grey trousers and a lightweight sweater. Lizzie had always said her cheater of an ex was a good-looking guy. Yeah. He could see that. The Frenchman was big with broad shoulders and a powerful body.

The first thing they did was kiss each other. Twice. Once on each cheek. Jesse knew that was the European way, but still he gripped tight onto the arms of the chair at the sight of Lizzie in an embrace with another guy. Not just another guy. The man she'd married, had intended to spend her life with, the father of her child. *Someone she'd loved.*

Ex-husband and ex-wife started to talk. Jesse hadn't hidden close enough to hear their actual words, just the sound of their voices. The conversation seemed to be more intense than angry with Philippe doing a lot of the talking. They were switching between English and French.

It was a shock to see Lizzie speaking French. She looked different—her mouth, her face— and she gesticulated with her hands in a Gallic way. This was a Lizzie who seemed to slip right back into a different persona altogether. It made him wonder how well he actually knew her.

He wished he'd sat closer so he could hear but he would have risked exposure. Was Philippe laying down terms for custody of Amy? Or was he putting his argument for his family to return to him in France? If the dude got angry with Lizzie, Jesse would be up there like a shot to protect her.

But, far from being an angry confrontation with her ex, Lizzie's meeting seemed amicable. Very amicable. *Too* amicable.

Lizzie smiled. She laughed. She *hugged* the guy who she'd told Jesse had made her life hell. The ex smiled too. He seemed too damn happy for a man who was being told his ex-wife would not give him custody of their daughter. Any sense of fun Jesse had felt in staking out Lizzie and her ex was quickly replaced by bitter disbelief.

There was too much laughter and good-will going on. Lizzie had said she dreaded the meeting but it looked to Jesse as if she was enjoying every minute of it.

Lizzie had problems with jealousy? Jesse had never before been bothered by it, had never understood the emotion. He sure as hell understood it now. Violent jealousy flamed through him at the sight of Lizzie with her ex-husband.

He felt excluded and it wasn't a feeling he liked. All the foundations he'd been building around Lizzie felt threatened.

They hugged *again*. Then they walked out to the lobby and towards the exit, chatting as they went.

Jesse got up from his lounge chair, slammed the newspaper on the table and headed towards the side door that led to the terrace. From there he would actually be able to hear their fare-wells unless Lizzie walked her ex to his rental car.

But no. They stayed put and did the one-kiss, two-kiss thing again. Then Lizzie looked up into her handsome ex-husband's face and said very clearly in English. 'I will see you in Lyon. For the start of a new life.'

Then she watched him get into the car and waved as he pulled out of the hotel driveway and headed north to Sydney.

Those final words reverberated through Jesse's mind. *I will see you in Lyon. For the start of a new life.*

What the hell had that meant? It was diffi-cult not to draw the obvious conclusion.

He'd been played for a fool again.

He wouldn't make the same mistake he'd made with Camilla. He was in deep with Lizzie, but he had an out. The job in Houston.

But first he'd give her a chance to explain herself. If she didn't come clean then he'd know he had been lied to again. That Lizzie intended to have her fun with him until it was time to go back to her other man. Like Camilla had.

His hands fisted by his sides, he stepped out from the terrace so Lizzie could see him as she approached.

Her face lit up when she saw him and she

hastened her steps to get to him quicker. It made his gut churn at how much he had come to care for her.

'So there you are,' she said. 'I've been looking for you. I've got good news.'

'Fire away,' he said gruffly.

'Philippe has dropped his plans to sue for sole custody. He flew all the way here to apologise about the way he behaved during our time together and to tell me—and to tell me…' She spluttered to a halt.

'To tell you what?' He felt choked by a grim foreboding.

'To…uh…to tell me how much he cared for Amy and how she would always be his first priority.'

She was lying. He couldn't fail to notice how she'd pulled herself up. No way would her ex come to the other side of the world just to tell her he was sorry for his behaviour of years ago. He believed the guy had apologised. But what had come next? Reconciliation? There'd been a lot of smiling and hugging. What the hell had that been about?

'That's good,' he muttered.

'You were a big hit with Amy, by the way, Uncle Jesse.' Lizzie chattered on, seemingly oblivious to his dark change of mood.

'Yeah, she's a great kid.' He'd been working at the café, educating Nikki in the finer aspects of pulling espresso shots, when Lizzie had brought Amy in to show her the café. Her little face had lit up when she'd seen him and she'd come tearing up to him to hurtle herself at him with a squeal of delight. 'Uncle Jesse!'

Laughing, he'd swept her up into his arms. It had taken him a long time after the fire to be comfortable around kids. He'd loved Ben's little boy Liam. It had seemed disloyal to pay attention to other children when his nephew had gone. He had taken his role as uncle very seriously. What role in his life might Amy play?

'Be flattered,' Lizzie had said. 'She doesn't take to everyone.'

'I wanted to introduce you to Philippe,' Lizzie said now.

He frowned. 'Why would you do that?'

So he'd be friendly to him when they got back together?

He thought back to one of the reasons he'd resisted pursuing Lizzie—if things went wrong he'd still have to see her at every family gathering. Her and her current man—perhaps her reconciled husband.

Not if he was in Houston, he wouldn't.

'Because, well, because he was here and because he's Amy's father I—'

'You told me how this guy cheated on you

and made your life hell. Why would I want to shake his hand?' He paused. 'Unless things have changed between you.'

She looked confused. 'Well, yes, they have changed.'

Here it came—the confession.

'What I meant is, *he's* changed. Grown up at last. Admitted his mistakes.'

'And?'

She frowned. 'What do you mean "and"? I don't know what you're talking about.'

'Haven't you got something to tell me?'

She flushed. 'Well, yes. I do.' She looked around her. 'But this isn't the time or the place to talk to you about it. What it means for us.'

He cursed inwardly. *So he hadn't misunderstood those overheard words.*

'There's something *I* need to tell *you*,' he said, unable to meet her eyes. 'The company in Houston contacted me this morning. They want a decision by close of business today and a start date of Monday if I accept. I'd have to leave Dolphin Bay tomorrow.'

The blood drained from her face. 'Oh,' she said. 'Wh-what will you do?'

'I'm going to take it.'

'Wh-what about your shoulder?'

'It's healed enough for desk duties.'

He hadn't meant to be so harsh about it.

Hadn't wanted to wound her. But hell, she had dealt him a body blow. Just like Camilla had.

'You'll be gone tomorrow?' Her voice was so faint he had to strain to hear it.

He nodded, unable to find the words that would take that stricken look off her face. Yet she still wouldn't admit she was going back to her husband. Or give him an explanation of why she'd lied. Why she had no explanation for those words he'd overheard.

He wanted to tell her he loved her. That he wanted to make decisions based on *their* future, not just his.

But she wasn't giving anything away. Not a word about her plans for going back to France to take up a new life with her old husband. Or why she was going to Lyon if it wasn't for that.

'So,' she said, with that familiar tilting of her chin. 'You'll be leaving Dolphin Bay?'

'Looks like it,' he said.

'Wh-what does that mean for us?' She turned her face away.

'You still don't have anything you want to tell me?' Anger and frustration and disbelief that he'd been caught again raged through him.

'It's not anything you'd want to hear,' she said in a very small voice.

That sealed it.

Then she met his gaze straight on. 'You'd better go make that phone call.'

She turned and he let her go.

CHAPTER FIFTEEN

LIZZIE WALKED AWAY from Jesse, expecting him to come after her. To tell her it was all a mistake. Reeling in shocked disbelief, she got halfway back to her apartment before she realised it wasn't going to happen. *Jesse had dumped her.* After all the emotional ups and downs she'd been through today, she was finding it impossible to stay steady on her feet. She had to stop and lean against one of the famous dolphin rubbish bins. Its smiling mouth seemed to mock her.

In a daze, she dragged her feet one step after another until she reached the door to her apartment and then hauled herself up the stairs.

The empty rooms derided her. Jesse was everywhere. His handprint all over the place—the tiles he'd laid, the walls he'd painted, the room he'd prepared for Amy. He was on the sofa where the aroma of peppermint still lingered. Most of all, he was in her bedroom.

How could he have made love to her with such tenderness and passion, only to dump her when her daughter came home?

Her heart contracted with the agony of the realisation of what it felt to be one of Jesse's disposable girls.

She'd cleared the bedroom of every trace of him so Amy wouldn't be aware Uncle Jesse had been sleeping over in Mummy's bed. She and Jesse had agreed it was too soon for her to know. She laid her head on the pillow where only this morning his beautiful dark head had rested. Where they had slept entwined in each other's arms. She lay where he had lain, breathed in deeply, hoping for a lingering trace of his scent but she'd stripped the bed and washed all the linen. There wasn't a trace of him left.

What had gone wrong?

He'd given her no clue. His change of heart had come completely out of the blue. Was it something to do with her meeting with Philippe? The meeting that had released her from the chains of resentment that had held her back from fully trusting Jesse.

The first thing Philippe had done was to apologise for the way he'd behaved during their marriage. Then he'd told her he was getting married again. To a French-Canadian girl named Thérèse who was also a chef.

Lizzie's first thought had been for Amy. But Philippe had reiterated his love for his daughter and said Thérèse wanted to be a good stepmother. In fact she wanted to meet Lizzie so she could discuss Amy's shared care when her little girl spent time in France. There was no longer any question that Philippe would seek sole custody.

For Amy's sake she had accepted the hand of reconciliation that Philippe had extended. 'We learn from our mistakes, yes?' Philippe had said.

She had agreed and, in doing so, had realised how unfair it had been of her to judge Jesse on the mistakes she had made with her ex-husband. *The men were nothing alike.*

Her relationship with Philippe had been founded on youthful passion fired by rebellion. She and her ex-husband had never been friends like Jesse and she had become. Jesse was both friend and lover—it was a formidable combination. She doubted her ex had understood her after several years together the way Jesse already understood her.

As she'd spoken with Philippe, something in her heart that had been frozen with bitterness and resentment had thawed. She'd felt freed from heavy chains she hadn't realised had been tethering her so tightly.

The revelation had had nothing to do with Philippe and everything to do with Jesse. Her feelings for him had changed everything. Had made her ready to forgive and move on with no lingering fears from the past to poison the present with jealousy and suspicion.

Jesse was the real deal. The happily ever after. The till death us do part.

Then she'd sought out Jesse, anxious to tell him what had happened—and to explain how the burden of Philippe's past behaviour had lifted so she was free to love again without the hindrance of bad old energy from the marriage gone wrong.

But Jesse had blocked her every way. Grim Jesse with the charming good looks gone dark and glowering. *Black Irish.* Jesse with the harsh voice, the eyes with the shutters suddenly down against her.

Jesse who, to all intents, had done exactly what she'd feared he'd do. *Made a conquest of her and then dumped her.* And boy had she been an easy conquest. She'd barely put up a struggle before she'd fallen so joyously into bed.

Just another of Jesse's girls after all. She'd believed she'd been so much more. How could

she have been so naïve, so stubborn, not to listen to her own sister's advice? She'd listened
to her heart instead and it had led her wrong.

And yet.

She'd grown to believe in Jesse so strongly
it was hard to let that trust go. She had truly
thought he wouldn't do this to her. But there
was no escaping that he had.

If she looked at it brutally, dispassionately,
the timing was right for him to get rid of her.
Amy had come home. With a five-year-old in
residence, they would have to snatch time together, might go days without intimacy. He
needed to free himself for new conquests.
Those Texan girls didn't know what they were
in for. Jesse the Player. Jesse the Heartbreaker.

She thought back, puzzling, seeking clues.
Philippe. It all came back to his visit. Maybe
Jesse was concerned about the ongoing contact with her ex-husband. There wasn't anything she could do about that. Amy deserved
to have a loving relationship with her father
and she was determined to facilitate that in
any way she could.

What had Jesse meant? He'd asked her if she
had something to tell him three times.

Did he want to know he had a place in her
and Amy's life when there was a father still
so actively involved with his daughter—even

though said father lived on the other side of the world?

Maybe Jesse wanted assurance.

Maybe Jesse wanted her to tell him how she felt.

Maybe she needed to tell Jesse she loved him, wanted him, would go to Houston with him. Would go anywhere with him—the Philippines, India, any old where. Because she realised with a huge whoosh of pain that made her double over with the agony of it that life without Jesse would be intolerable.

She got up from the bed. She had to find him. Tell him she loved him. And if it all blew up in her face, if she was after all the latest in a long line of discarded Jesse's girls, at least she would have tried.

She clattered down the stairs of her apartment, waved to one of the waitresses who stood outside the door of the café talking on her phone. She kept her demeanour calm, her face controlled. As far as anyone else in Dolphin Bay knew, she and Jesse were just friends. It wouldn't look right for her to be stressed and tearful and hunting around town for him.

But where could she find him?

She didn't want to call him on his mobile phone to alert him she was coming after him.

She went to the boathouse. No Jesse. His car was gone too.

If Jesse was indeed taking off for Texas tomorrow, surely he'd want a farewell swim at his favourite beach. She'd take a punt he'd gone to Silver Gull. If he hadn't gone there she'd keep on looking until she found him. Even if she had to drive to Sydney and confront him at the airport.

No way was she going to let Jesse go until she'd made absolutely sure there was no hope left for them.

Jesse swam up and down the length of the beach, churning through the freezing water until his shoulder ached too much to go on. He'd had to fight a strong swell to get out beyond the breaking waves. That was nothing to the fight he'd had against himself. But the salt water and the vigorous exercise had cleared his head.

He'd been an idiot. The worst of the wussies. He'd let all the pain and fear from his early decision to avoid love make him act like an irrational, bad-tempered fool. He'd let the pain of Camilla's old betrayal blind him to the fact that Lizzie was not Camilla. Lizzie had not set out to hurt him. *He had hurt her.*

While he'd raged against the idea that Lizzie

was going back to her ex-husband, she had never actually said she was. Remembering the bewildered look on her lovely face made him realise his anger had stopped him thinking straight.

Now he understood what Lizzie had struggled with—jealousy could turn a person crazy.

He should have asked Lizzie outright about what he'd overheard. Instead he'd set her a test of honesty she hadn't even known she had to pass. He'd been totally out of order. Cruel. Cowardly. Worse, he had betrayed the trust she'd worked so hard to build up from a baseline of emotional abuse.

He strode out of the water. Slung a towel around him and headed towards his car. He had to find her. Grovel. Apologise. Grovel some more. *Tell her how much he cared for her.*

Only to see Lizzie walking across the sand towards him. Her face was a mass of contradictions. Fear. Determination. And something else shining from her eyes that made his heart leap inside his chest.

He ran to meet her. But as he got closer she put up her hand to stop him. 'Before you come any further, Jesse Morgan, I want to answer that question you kept asking me before—have I got anything to tell you?'

He groaned. 'That was a mistake. I—' But she spoke right over him in that blunt, determined Lizzie way.

'I *have* got something to tell you. I don't know if it's what you wanted to hear but you're going to hear it anyway. I love you, Jesse. I fancied you the moment I met you. Then I fell in love with you when you danced me around a deserted beach in the moonlight to the sound of the stars. Or maybe when you massaged my feet. It could even have been when you pulled coffees all day just to help me out. Whatever. I nearly lost you the first time through a silly misunderstanding and I don't want to lose you again through another one. Is that what you wanted me to tell you?'

Her eyes were huge and her mouth quivered as she waited for his answer.

She loved him.

How could he have been such an idiot as to risk losing her?

He wanted to pull her into his arms and tell her he loved her too and that she was the most amazing woman he'd ever met. That she had become his favourite person in the whole world. That it would be like wrenching out his soul if he couldn't have her in his life. But that was beyond his limited skills as an orator. And he feared she wouldn't welcome his touch. Especially as he was dripping salt water.

'No, it wasn't,' he said. 'You gave me a better answer.'

'What do you mean?' she said, hope struggling to life amid the woeful expression on her face. 'You're talking in riddles, Jesse, and I'm in no mood to try to solve them.'

He took a deep breath. 'I overheard you talking to your ex. You hugged him, kissed him and said: "I will see you in Lyon. For the start of a new life."'

Why the hell hadn't he asked her that directly?

She frowned. 'You were there? Listening?'

'I heard every word of your farewell. Then, when we met up afterwards, I wanted you to tell me what you had meant by that promise to see him in Lyon. Did it mean you were going back to him? That's the conclusion I jumped to. But if you say you love me, I guess you won't be boarding a plane to France any time soon.'

She crossed her arms in front of her. 'I certainly won't be going back to Philippe. That was never, ever on the cards. Why didn't you just ask me?'

'Because I was a stupid, insecure idiot, too blinded by fear of losing you to think straight.

So I'll ask you now. Why *are* you going to France to see your ex-husband?'

'You might be going too,' she said.

'Now you're the one talking in riddles.'

'Let me explain,' she said, uncrossing her arms.

'Please do,' he said. *Man, had he made a mess of this.*

'Philippe asked me to keep this secret for Amy's sake. But you're more important than keeping his confidence. He's getting married and his fiancée wants me and Amy to be there at the wedding next April in Lyon. You're invited too. Actually, I invited you. But Philippe didn't want Amy to know until closer to the time and he asked me not to tell anyone in case she overheard.'

'Your ex is getting married?' That was the last thing he had expected to hear.

'Is it so surprising? People do get remarried, you know. And I'm happy for him.'

'I thought he wanted you back.'

Now her eyes were accusing. 'How could you possibly think I'd go back to him after what you and I have shared together? The... the fairy tale magic. What kind of a woman do you think I am?'

'Obviously one I'm not worthy of,' he said slowly. He tasted regret, bitter and stinging.

All her indignation and anger fled from her face and her eyes softened. She reached up and laid her fingers across his mouth. 'Oh, Jesse, don't say that. After all we've been through to get here.'

He took her fingers in his hand. 'Can you forgive me?'

'If you'll forgive me for keeping secrets from you. I should have told you straight away about the wedding in Lyon. I love you, Jesse. I couldn't bear to lose you.'

Relief swelled through him. 'That's twice you've told me you love me. Can you give a man a chance to catch up?'

He couldn't wait another second to gather her close to him. She squealed. 'You're wet and cold but I don't care.'

He claimed her mouth in a kiss. 'I love you, Lizzie,' he said, revelling in the sound of the words and how it made him feel to say them. 'I love you, Lizzie,' he repeated. 'That's twice I've said it. We're even.'

She locked her arms around his neck. 'I'm going to tell you how much I love you a lot more times than that. I'm coming to Texas with you. Amy too.'

'You'd leave the café?'

'Funnily enough, though it didn't seem the best job in the world when I came down to

Dolphin Bay, I've got attached to it. But not as attached as I am to you. So yes, I'll leave it after training someone else to take over so I don't let Sandy down.'

'You don't have to leave. I'm staying right here in Dolphin Bay.'

'What do you mean?'

'I'm going into business with Ben.'

She frowned. 'Is it what you really want? You're not compromising for my sake? Because if—'

'It's what I really want. I want you too. No more pretending to be "just friends" either. No more being jealous because we're not certain of each other.'

'Jealous? You?'

'You turned me into a jealous guy when I saw you hugging and kissing Philippe.'

She shrugged in that Gallic way. 'It's just a French thing. The kissing. Nothing to be concerned about.'

'I didn't like it.'

'So we're both jealous. Do two people being jealous cancel out the jealousy?'

She was making light of it. But he knew how concerned she was about her jealousy causing problems.

'I have a better idea,' he said. 'Love. Security. Commitment. Knowing the other person is always in your court. That could go a long way to cancelling out the jealousy.'

She went very still. He was aware of the sound of the waves. The thudding of his own heart. 'I...I'm not sure what you're getting at,' she said.

He'd thought about this when he'd been swimming up and down in the surf. How he couldn't bear to be without Lizzie in his life. How he could think of nothing better than making her and Amy his family. How what she needed had become what he needed. 'A wedding ring firmly circling your finger is my idea of a jealousy buster,' he said.

'And a matching one circling yours is mine,' she said. Her wonderful warm laugh rang out across the beach. 'Did you just propose to me, Jesse Morgan?'

'Did you just accept my proposal, Lizzie Morgan to-be?'

'I did,' she said, planting a kiss on his mouth. 'And...and I couldn't be happier.'

'Me too,' he said and kissed her back. His heart actually ached with joy.

She broke away from the kiss. 'You realise there will be a lot of upset people in town when this news leaks out?'

'Who? My family will be delighted.'

'The punters who laid bets you'd never marry.'

'Serves them right for giving you the wrong impression of me and making it so tough for me to win you.'

She smiled. 'I'm glad you changed my mind about that. I love you, Jesse.'

'I love you too,' he said. 'That makes three times we've said it.'

'Shall we try for thirty times before the day is over?'

'Why not?' he said. 'I'll never tire of hearing those words from you.'

EPILOGUE

Two months later

AS A CHILD, Christmas had not been Lizzie's favourite time of year—her family Christmas Days had always seen the sad cliché of every bitterness and conflict getting a good airing over the roast turkey and plum pudding.

As an adult, she had embraced Christmas as a joyous celebration, growing to love festive traditions whether celebrated in the winter of Europe or the Australian summer.

But this year's Christmas was going to be the most magical and memorable of all—because this year Lizzie was celebrating Christmas as a bride.

On Christmas Eve—a perfect sunny south coast morning—Lizzie let Sandy fuss around fixing her hair, which had been braided into a thick plait interwoven with white ribbons and creamy frangipani flowers. In her ears were the exquisite diamond studs Jesse had given her as an early Christmas present.

The sisters were getting ready in a location van parked on the approach to Silver Gull beach. As the most significant moments of their courtship had taken place on beaches, she and Jesse had decided Silver Gull would be the perfect venue for their exchange of vows.

The location van had been Sandy's idea; she was familiar with such luxuries from her days working on advertising shoots. Lizzie marvelled at the set-up—the interior was like a dressing room complete with mirrors and even a small bathroom. It was the ideal place to prepare for a wedding at a beach.

'Now, let me check the dress,' said Sandy, who was taking her duties as Lizzie's bridesmaid very seriously.

Lizzie was so happy to be getting married to Jesse she hadn't imagined she'd be plagued by any wedding day nerves. Not so. She wasn't worried about the details of the ceremony; they had all been organised by Kate Lancaster, who had done such a marvellous job as wedding planner for Sandy and Ben's wedding. Or about the reception—a small informal affair which was to be held back at Bay Bites. Lizzie's team had all that under control.

No. Lizzie's concern was that she wanted to look beautiful for Jesse.

She did a twirl as best she could in the confines of the van. 'Do you think Jesse will like it?' she asked Sandy, unable to suppress the tremor in her voice. She loved the ankle-length dress for its elegant simplicity: a V-neck tunic in soft off-white tulle lace layered over a silk under-dress and caught in with a flat bow in the small of her back.

'Jesse won't be able to keep his eyes off you,' said Sandy. 'I've never seen a lovelier bride, and I'm not saying that because you're my baby sister. That dress is divine—simple, elegant, discreetly sexy. Just like you.'

Lizzie hugged her. 'You're okay about me marrying Jesse, aren't you?' she asked. 'You warned me off him so many times. But he isn't what people said, you know. He makes me happier than I ever could have imagined.'

She was taken aback by Sandy's burst of laughter. 'Ben and I couldn't be more delighted you two are getting married. You and Jesse are perfect for each other. But you're so stubborn you would have run the other way if I'd told you that. You had to find each other in your own way.'

Lizzie's first reaction was to huff indignantly. But instead she smiled. 'You did me a favour and I'm grateful.' She paused. 'Sisters married to brothers. It's worked out so well for us, hasn't it? Our guys from Dolphin Bay.'

'Yes,' said Sandy. Her hand went protectively to the slight swell of her belly. She and Ben were expecting a baby in six months' time—an event anticipated with much joy by the Morgan clan. 'We're both getting our happily-ever-after endings.'

Then Sandy bustled Lizzie towards the door of the van. 'Come on, bride, your gorgeous groom is waiting for you.'

Lizzie waited at the start of the 'aisle' formed by double rows of seashells that led to a white wooden wedding arch adorned with filmy white fabric and sprays of the small red flowers of the New South Wales Christmas bush. The aquamarine waters of the ocean with the white waves rolling in formed the most glorious backdrop for her wedding ceremony. When she drew in some deep calming breaths, the salt smell of the sea mingled with the sweet scent of the frangipani in her hair.

Both Sandy and Amy, her only attendants, had preceded her down the aisle. They both wore pretty knee-length dresses in a shade of palest coffee. Barista coffee, Lizzie had joked. They were all barefoot, with their toe-nails painted Christmas red in honour of the festive season.

There was one more thing to do before Lizzie took her journey down the aisle. She laid aside her bouquet of Christmas bush. Then slipped off her diamond engagement ring from the third finger of her left hand and transferred it to her right hand. Jesse had surprised her with the superb solitaire in a starkly simple platinum setting just days after he had proposed to her on this very beach.

She watched as Sandy reached the wedding arch and took her place beside Ben, Jesse's best man. On her other side, Amy held her aunt's hand. Then it was Lizzie's turn to walk down the aisle to get married to Jesse.

The sand either side of the aisle was lined with well-wishers but they were just a blur to Lizzie. She recognised Maura standing by with Amy's adored Alfie and Ben's golden retriever Hobo firmly secured by leashes. But the only face she wanted to see was Jesse's.

And then she was beside him; he was clean-shaven, his black hair tamed, heart-achingly handsome in a stone-coloured linen suit and an open-neck white silk shirt. Any doubts she might have had about him finding her beautiful on her wedding day were dispersed by the look of adoration in his deep blue eyes as he took her hand in his and drew her to his side.

'I love you,' he murmured.

'I love you too,' she whispered.

'That's three thousand and sixty-three times we've said it,' he said.

'And we have a lifetime ahead of us to keep on saying it,' she said, tightening her clasp on his hand.

The celebrant called the guests to order. Before she knew it, they'd exchanged vows and Jesse was slipping the platinum wedding ring on her finger and then her diamond ring on top. 'I declare you man and wife,' said the celebrant.

'Now I can kiss my bride,' said Jesse, gathering her into his arms. 'Mrs Lizzie Morgan.'

Their kiss should have been the cue for classical wedding music to play through the speakers placed strategically near the wedding arch.

But, as Jesse claimed his first kiss as her husband, Lizzie was stunned to hear instead the distinctive notes of Jesse's signature tune rearranged for violin and piano.

'Where did that music come from?' she asked Jesse.

Jesse laughed. 'No idea. But I like it. Now

you truly are Jesse's girl.' He kissed her again to the accompaniment of clapping and cheering from their friends and family. 'My wife— the best Christmas present ever.'

* * * * *

LARGER-PRINT BOOKS!
GET 2 FREE LARGER-PRINT NOVELS PLUS
2 FREE GIFTS!

HARLEQUIN®

Romance

From the Heart, For the Heart

YES! Please send me 2 FREE LARGER-PRINT Harlequin® Romance novels and my 2 FREE gifts (gifts are worth about $10). After receiving them, if I don't wish to receive any more books, I can return the shipping statement marked "cancel." If I don't cancel, I will receive 4 brand-new novels every month and be billed just $4.84 per book in the U.S. or $5.24 per book in Canada. That's a savings of at least 19% off the cover price! It's quite a bargain! Shipping and handling is just 50¢ per book in the U.S. and 75¢ per book in Canada.* I understand that accepting the 2 free books and gifts places me under no obligation to buy anything. I can always return a shipment and cancel at any time. Even if I never buy another book, the two free books and gifts are mine to keep forever.

119/319 HDN F43Y

Name _____ (PLEASE PRINT) _____

Address _____ Apt. # _____

City _____ State/Prov. _____ Zip/Postal Code _____

Signature (if under 18, a parent or guardian must sign) _____

Mail to the **Harlequin® Reader Service:**
IN U.S.A.: P.O. Box 1867, Buffalo, NY 14240-1867
IN CANADA: P.O. Box 609, Fort Erie, Ontario L2A 5X3
Want to try two free books from another line?
Call 1-800-873-8635 or visit www.ReaderService.com.

* Terms and prices subject to change without notice. Prices do not include applicable taxes. Sales tax applicable in N.Y. Canadian residents will be charged applicable taxes. Offer not valid in Quebec. This offer is limited to one order per household. Not valid for current subscribers to Harlequin Romance Larger-Print books. All orders subject to credit approval. Credit or debit balances in a customer's account(s) may be offset by any other outstanding balance owed by or to the customer. Please allow 4 to 6 weeks for delivery. Offer available while quantities last.

Your Privacy—The Harlequin® Reader Service is committed to protecting your privacy. Our Privacy Policy is available online at www.ReaderService.com or upon request from the Harlequin Reader Service.

We make a portion of our mailing list available to reputable third parties that offer products we believe may interest you. If you prefer that we not exchange your name with third parties, or if you wish to clarify or modify your communication preferences, please visit us at www.ReaderService.com/consumerschoice or write to us at Harlequin Reader Service Preference Service, P.O. Box 9062, Buffalo, NY 14269. Include your complete name and address.

HRLP13R

SPECIAL EXCERPT FROM

*Read on for an enticing taster of
Rebecca Winters's next book,
TAMING THE FRENCH TYCOON:*

THIS TIME SHE searched for his mouth with stunning impatience, telling him without words. Their kiss went on and on until he felt transported.

But a different kind of pain than he'd known before shot through him because this was her goodbye kiss. He pulled her right up against his chest and buried his face in her neck. She really was going away. This wasn't something he could talk her out of.

"Jasmine? Before you leave for the States, I have to spend some time with you. I'll take my vacation now. How soon do you have to go?"

"I promised to be home on August 7. It's my parents' thirtieth wedding anniversary party."

So soon? Everything in him rebelled. His mind calculated the time. "That gives us a week."

A moan sounded before she moved off his lap and stood up. "No more make believe, Luc. I couldn't go anywhere with you."

He stared up at her. "Why not?"

"You *know* why. Your life is here. Mine is on the other side of the Atlantic. How could it possibly be good for either of us to go off for that long, knowing we're going to say goodbye at the end? The thought of it is too painful to even contemplate." Her voice throbbed. "At least it is for me. But you're a man, so it's different for you."

"Explain that remark."

Jasmine wouldn't look at him. "You can go away with a woman and enjoy the time thoroughly. When it's over you can move on. But women are different. Not all, but some. *I'm* different. To travel and make love with you, only to get on a plane at the end of that journey and wave goodbye sounds like a kind of purgatory I have no desire to live through."

He grasped her hand. "Then we won't sleep together."

She looked down at him and smiled. "You're a Frenchman aren't you?"

"I'm a man like all other men, and the thought of making love to you has been on my mind since I saw you on Yeronisos. But that isn't why I want to go away with you. If you think making love to you is all I'm after, then you have an odd conception about me.

"The other day I told you I have feelings for you I've never had for another woman. If all I can do is hold you and kiss you while we're on vacation, it will be enough. What I'd truly regret is not being able to get to know Jasmine Martin, the fabulous woman inside the girl who makes me want to be a better man."